Firmament:
Radialloy

Firmament:
Radialloy

by J. Grace Pennington

For Hope, my beloved Watson
Because she's my biggest fan.

SPECIAL THANKS

First, I'd like to thank my family, who bore with me through the long hours of writing, revising, and brainstorming for this book. In addition to that, my sister Hope read every chapter as it left my keyboard, my brother Jacob helped me brainstorm and created my beautiful cover, and my sisters Faith and Patience were faithful and patient readers. And especially my parents, who have supported my writing all through the years.

Second, I want to thank my test readers; Aubrey Hansen, Katie Lynn Daniels, Jonathan Garner, Shanalyse Barnett, Jenni Noordhoek, Carolyn Noordhoek, Megan Langham, Jeffrey French, and Lawrence Mark Coddington. Each of you has shaped this book in very special ways, and I am grateful for your contributions.

Also worth thanking are my wonderful "pokers," who kept me accountable even though they had not read the book. There are too many to list here, but among the most persistent were Kaitlyn Emery, Matthew Schleusener, and P. Rose Williams.

I'd also like to thank A. Andrew Joyce for creating the starmap that numbered all my sectors, Earl Merritt Jr., M.D. for checking medical details, Carolyn Noordhoek for designing Andi's beautiful uniform, Matthew Sample II for critiquing the cover, and the members of HolyWorlds Sci-Fi forum for brainstorming so much of the technology with me.

Most of all, I thank my Lord Jesus Christ for giving me the dream, desire, and talent to do this, and for placing this story in my heart and giving me the strength to persevere with it to the end.

CHAPTER I

He always said that I had the measles when he found me on his doorstep back in 2299, and he also said that I was less than a year old. I believed him, because first of all he was a doctor and ought to know about such things, and secondly, I would have had to be a pretty pitiful sight to induce him to take me in.

He also said that it wasn't until he'd nursed me through the measles that it even occurred to him to keep me. That made sense also, given his status as a rather private bachelor with a small practice in Grand Forks, North Dakota. Adopting little orphan girls with measles probably wasn't something he'd planned on doing, but he didn't seem sorry that he'd found me. I know I wasn't.

He also probably hadn't planned on going to space ten years later, but he didn't seem sorry about that, either. I knew he'd had his doubts at first, but he'd felt it was the right thing to do.

Since I'd spent half my life in space, it was more like home than Earth was. Our home now was the *Surveyor*, a class-A vessel, who, like the late-twentieth-century probes whose name she bore, was assigned to explore, document, and inform. Specifically, to search the outer reaches of the galaxy and beyond for alien life forms. Here, we had friends, plenty of everything, and I could be with the Doctor and help him with his work all I wanted.

"Andi, where'd you put the new instrument?" he called to me from sickbay.

"You mean the compact magnetic resonance scanner?" I yelled back. I hurried to finish washing my hands.

He stepped into the long, clean, starkly white sanitation room, where I was blowing my hands dry, his thin form framed in the center of the metal doorway. "That's not very funny."

"It wasn't meant to be funny, that's what it's called."

Not knowing a good answer for that, he eyed the dryer I had been using. "You'd think that in the last three hundred years they would have invented something better than that for hand drying. Those things have been around forever."

"So have you, and I like you just fine." I smiled mischievously as I approached him.

He glared at me, clearly trying to decide how to take that. But at last he smiled, and then laughed, and then patted me on the shoulder. "I suppose I should be grateful for that."

"You might as well," I laughed back. I surveyed him, and then reached up to adjust his collar, which was folded under slightly. "The new uniform looks really nice."

"It's too stiff," he grunted. "I don't know why they have to change regulations constantly. Green isn't my color."

I smiled. Green was the absolute perfect color to go with his delightfully deep gray eyes and his iron gray hair. I smoothed the front of my own jacket with a hint of self-consciousness.

"How does mine look?" I wasn't sure fair skin, honey-golden hair and brown eyes would go with the forest green.

His expression changed to a rare, warm smile. "You look fine."

The "fine" meant more coming from him than "beautiful" would have meant from anyone else. I smiled at him.

He grunted a bit. "All right. Now tell me where that scanner is."

I hurried out into sickbay to get it, taking in the bright whiteness of the room, the comforting hum of the monitors and the slight scent of drugs and sanitizer with a happy sigh. This place never got old for me.

When I reached the main medical supply cabinet on the opposite side of the room, I opened the white metal doors and pulled the tiny, cylindrical scanner off the shelf. "Here it is, Doctor."

He took it from me, looking it over skeptically. "You sure

this thing is an improvement? Looks pretty strange to me. I liked the old scanner just fine."

I closed the cabinet. "I haven't worked with it that much yet, but I like it."

He tossed it in the air a couple of times. "Pretty small. These things took up a whole room when I was in in medical school."

"Yes, they use directed safe radiation to strengthen the magnet. I read about it."

He raised one eyebrow. "Radiation?"

"It's safe and easy to use, Doctor, don't worry. It works pretty much just like the old MCT scanner."

"Yes, but I just got used to that one. I don't see why they're always inventing new things."

"You were just criticizing 'them' for *not* inventing a new hand dryer." I couldn't help it, I really couldn't. It did seem to annoy him a bit this time.

"Well you can tell them from me to stop inventing new scanners, and start on the hand dryers. Now come on, Andi, I need your help."

"Yes sir."

Following him between the two long rows of cots that lined the walls of sickbay, I chuckled to myself. I remembered the first time I'd called him "Doctor" at age nine. It had been a pert joke about his tendency to give me work to do as if I were a nurse. He'd raised his eyebrows at me then, but it had stuck and become habit for both of us.

"What do you want me to do?" I asked dutifully.

Leaning over a patient and connecting the scanner, he pointed over his shoulder towards a young man who lay on a cot on the other side of the room. "Take care of him."

I reached into a white box that hung on the wall and pulled out a pair of rubber gloves. Snapping them on, I moved over to the person he had indicated.

It was a young lieutenant, I observed by the insignia etched on his metal arm band. Although the *Surveyor* was a private ship, rather than one of the few military vessels, she still followed the traditional ranking system of captain, commander, lieutenant, etc. I'd asked why once and the Captain had explained that there had to be some rank, or how would anyone know who was in charge?

I frowned at the armband as I approached. The Doctor was opposed to them as a general rule—said they restricted a patient's circulation. He had frustrated the Captain when we first came aboard by refusing to wear one himself or allow me to wear one. They had compromised by deciding that we would wear cloth bands instead. If the Doctor had gotten to this young man first, the wide, white band would have been removed from his upper arm before he had time to even think about it.

The patient's eyes were closed as I approached him, and I took the opportunity to observe him. I didn't know who he was, which puzzled me, since I knew all one-hundred and twelve people on the ship by sight at least. He was about twenty-five, I guessed, clean-shaven and average height with regular features and dark brown hair.

I punched my authorization code into his monitor so I could read his status and the beeping attracted his attention.

"Who are you?"

He had some kind of accent, one I'd never heard before. Not that that meant much, I hadn't heard many accents in my days. Most people on the ship were American, and in the collective two or three weeks a year I spent back on Earth I never had much opportunity to meet other people.

"I'm the Doctor's assistant." I selected the "case history" tab on the screen before turning to face him. "Did you just come in?"

"A minute ago."

"That explains it." I put my hand under his elbow and clicked open the armband. "This should have come off right away."

"Hey..."

"No heys. With such low blood pressure, you shouldn't

even be wearing one of these. I'm going to have to have a talk with Captain Trent about this."

I deposited the armband in the Personal Effects Box which hung just below the cot.

"How long have you been subject to hypotension?" I questioned, pulling out a bottle of crystalloid tablets from that station's medicine cabinet.

"What, you mean my low blood pressure?"

"That is the general meaning of the word hypotension." I took secret joy in flaunting my medical knowledge to the uninitiated. "You get lightheaded and exhausted when you move too much or change quickly from one position to another, correct?"

"Yes. I was just going to rest, but Captain Trent said..."

"Captain Trent was right." I handed him the pills and a glass of water, and he took them meekly, still eyeing me.

"What's your name?" he asked.

"Andi Lloyd."

"Any relation to Doctor Lloyd?"

"He's my father." I poured a few drops of Enari into a bottle of water, closed it and shook hit well. "Drink this after your next meal, and drink at least sixty-four ounces of water a day. Notify the Doctor immediately if it happens again within forty-eight hours."

The lieutenant took the bottle, still staring at me. Then he looked at the Doctor, who was patching up a patient's hand on the other side of the room.

"You don't look much alike," was his casual comment.

"No, we don't." I wasn't interested in explaining the relationship to someone I didn't even know. "You can leave now, just rest for about two hours, and I advise you not to put that armband back on."

"Thank you," seemed to be all he could think of to say. "Goodbye." Standing up, he took the armband out of the box and held it between two fingers. "By the way, my name's August

Howitz. I'm the new navigator."

"Goodbye, August Howitz. Have fun navigating."

I wasn't sure what he'd think of this, but he smiled and nodded, then gave his bottle a good shake before leaving the facility.

I turned off the monitor, stripped the sheets from the cot he'd lain on, and tossed them into the laundry chute, then replaced them with fresh ones. I stretched and yawned, glancing around the room for patients. There were none, and I tripped over to the Doctor, who was straightening some supplies.

"Can I go help with lunch?"

"All right," he nodded. "I'll be down in a while."

I glanced at my wristcom to see the time as I walked out into the bright, white halls. Eleven. Much of the crew would already be down there, maybe even the Captain, and his first officer, Guilders. They usually made their trip down there around eleven. I quickened my steps, hoping to be in time to help the cook.

The mess hall was on the other side of the ship from sickbay, so it took me a few minutes to get there. As I approached the tall, wide doorway, the talking and laughing told me that a generous crowd had already accumulated there. No doubt Almira would appreciate my help today.

I slipped in and glanced around to gauge how many had arrived. About forty, I thought, which left the fifty members of the night crew and about twenty who were still at their posts. Yes, the Captain and Guilders were there, at their usual table in the far corner, though there was a stranger with them. I couldn't place him, but he seemed vaguely familiar.

"Andi!" a young male voice called. I turned to see Edwardo, a galley assistant, carrying a tray nearby. "You here to eat or to help out?"

"I'm helping for a minute," I said. "You can go ahead and eat if you want."

"Gracias!" he smiled, then hurried to his destination.

I wove through the tables toward the snack bar and galley, sniffing the fresh scent of hot tomato soup as I passed the diners. The mess hall was not white and sterile like sickbay. It was warm and brown and, in a way, homey. Just like Almira.

She was bending over a pot on the stove as I entered, her black face dotted with little bits of perspiration. A simple, flowered apron was tied around her generous middle, clashing cheerfully with the green jacket, and her black hair was pulled up in that familiar knot behind her head.

She turned as I walked forward. "Edwardo, is that..." she began. "Why Andi!" She left the pot and pulled one of her big aprons out of a silver metal drawer. "So nice of you to come help out, honey! And the new uniform—why, it's just your color!"

I smiled, and lifted my arms to let her tie the apron on. "Too nice to get tomato soup on I suppose. Thank you."

"Yes indeed," she smiled. "Would you mind stirring for me?"

I washed my hands, then began to stir the heavenly smelling brew while she bustled about getting out other food. "I thought you'd be helping your daddy this time of day?"

"There weren't many patients." I brushed a bit of hair behind my ear and kept stirring. "Did you see the man sitting with the Captain and Guilders?"

"I haven't been out there. What man?"

I shrugged, watching reddish-white bubbles form and pop as the soup boiled. "I don't know. I don't think I know him. And there was another man in sickbay earlier that I didn't know."

"Oh, that would be Commander Howitz and his son," she said, laying out a few rows of plates and putting bread on each one. "They're new—only been here a couple weeks."

"New? But how did they join in the middle of a flight? We've been away from Earth for—" I calculated. "Three months."

"I don't know. But they seem like nice gentlemen." She was quiet as she finished distributing the bread. "Is that done?"

"I don't know." I handed the spoon to her and stepped

aside. After sniffing it, she picked up a clean spoon and dipped it into the pot, then took a sip. She nodded. "Done."

"Do you want me to serve?" I went ahead and started untying my apron.

"Yes, thank you, honey. This is the last round, then you can go eat if you like."

She filled each bowl to the brim, setting each one on a plate with bread, and then I put each plate on the tray. When the tray was full, I sauntered out to deliver the meals to the hungry crewmen closest to the galley, then went back for the last trip.

The only people left without food were the Captain and those at his table. I saw Guilders, and the new man—Commander Howitz, Almira had said—and someone else. It looked like—yes, it was Lieutenant Howitz, who I'd examined earlier.

The Captain and Commander Howitz were laughing over their drinks, and the other two men sat more quietly. As I approached the table, the Captain looked up and smiled at me. "Andi! Gerry said you were down here."

"Hello, Captain." I put a plate down in front of him. He always impressed me like the sea captains I'd read about as a child—tall, masculine, with a bronzed face and a cheerful smile for everyone.

"Have you met our new navigator?" he asked, with a familiar twinkle in his eye, gesturing towards Lieutenant Howitz.

I looked at the young man and sighed inwardly. If I had a dollar for every time the Captain had tried to set me up with some young crewman, I could refurbish the entire sickbay, at least. "Yes, I meant to talk to you about him, Captain," I said. "I told him not to wear his armband anymore, his blood pressure is too low."

Lieutenant Howitz reddened and slipped his right hand over the band. His father laughed.

"Oh come now, Andi..." the Captain began.

"Oh come now, Captain, you know the Doctor's been telling you the problems for years."

He laughed. "I'll have a talk with Gerry about it."

"You'll never agree." I put another plate in front of Commander Howitz, who nodded his thanks with a broad smile.

"If we agreed, what fun would we have?" His blue eyes twinkled.

I shook my head with a smile, and handed a plate to Lieutenant Howitz, who nodded. There were three more plates, and I gave one to Guilders.

"Thank you," he said in his low-pitched voice, with just a hint of a smile.

I set the other two plates down and started to raise my wristcom to my mouth, when the Captain interrupted me.

"I already called him, Andi. He's on his way down."

"All right." I slid into a seat opposite young Lieutenant Howitz and began to eat. He nodded politely at me, but didn't speak.

After a taking a few spoonfuls of soup, Commander Howitz wiped his mouth, and stuck his large hand towards me with a broad smile. "Hello. I'm Erasmus Howitz," he said in a low, gravelly voice.

I shook his hand. "I'm Andi Lloyd." His features and hair were much like August's, but he was much bigger and more imposing. August had more of a shy, polite air. "You're new here?"

The Captain looked at me. "Commander Howitz is our new engineer. I've heard wonderful things about him."

"Good," was the only thing I could think of to say. *Come on, Andi! Talk!*

I turned to Guilders for relief, as I often did. Guilders was a comforting person. The ship's helmsman since her maiden voyage, he was close to sixty years old, and had been aboard longer than anyone else. His calm, solid face with the white, bushy eyebrows seemed as much a part of the ship as the bridge, or the thrusters, or the airlocks. "How have things been on the bridge, Mr. Guilders?"

"Everything has been as usual," he said, going on with his meal. "You have not visited us there for awhile, Miss Andi."

"No," I apologized. "We've been busier than usual."

"You don't work on the bridge, then?" Commander Howitz asked.

"Oh no. But I do enjoy visiting there." I flashed a smile at the Captain. Sometimes he even asked me to substitute for some of the bridge positions, which I enjoyed in moderation, though I refused to give in to his suggestions of permanent appointment to any of them. I was only interested in helping the Doctor.

"Ever visit engineering?" the Commander asked, continuing to eat his soup.

He seemed nice and friendly—I just wished he didn't have such a gravelly voice. It made me feel uncomfortable and tongue-tied.

"No, I'm not supposed to go there."

He eyed me quizzically, and I gave a little laugh. "It's not—I mean, it's just because I have metal in my kneecap. People with metal implants aren't supposed to go down to engineering, because of the radiation."

"I see." He didn't sound interested, and just stared into his soup as I spoke. But when he looked up a moment later, his eyes had an inquisitive glint. "Forgive my curiosity—as a scientist, I've always been interested in prosthetics. What metal is it?"

I shrugged my shoulders. "I don't know."

He nodded, and went back to his food.

"Eating without me?" I heard the Doctor's voice say, as he sat down beside me. "I see Almira's still up to her old tricks."

"Tricks?" the Captain asked.

"A tomato a day keeps the doctor away."

I grinned. "That's apples, Dad."

"I don't mind apples," he protested. "It's those squishy red... things."

"It's good," I coaxed.

With a sigh, he picked up his spoon.

"Doctor Lloyd?" Commander Howitz half-stated.

The Doctor looked up. "I'm Doctor Lloyd. Who are you?"

"Commander Howitz. My son and I are new here."

"Ah, your son of the orthostatic hypotension?" The Doctor whisked a spoonful into his mouth as he nodded at August.

"I beg your pardon?"

The Captain's wristcom beeped just then, and he pushed a button to answer it. "Trent here."

"Captain, we're receiving a mooring request."

"I'll be right there." He took his finger off the button, and stood up. "Officers to the bridge."

August and Guilders stood, but I spoke up quickly. "Captain, Lieutenant Howitz needs his rest."

The Captain glanced at the navigator, who said nothing.

"Very well. Can you substitute?"

"Yes sir." I popped a last bite of bread in my mouth, took a quick swig of water, and then stood up, laying a hand on the Doctor's back affectionately. "I'll see you later."

He nodded, still trying to down the tomato soup, and I followed the Captain and Guilders up to the bridge.

CHAPTER II

A short walk and an elevator ride later, we were entering that center of control that I always loved to visit. As the doors slid open, I stepped into the spacious, open room, with windows spanning three walls along the fore and sides. The colors, a pleasing, mellow blue and gray, harmonized with the deep green jackets of the three primary officers who had remained in their stations. The data controller and the comm marshal sat at their panels, while the science exec had the captain's chair.

He arose as we entered, and faced his captain.

"Mr. Yanendale marshaled the message, sir."

"Identification?" the Captain asked, settling himself in his accustomed seat.

"None yet, sir. We notified you first."

Guilders headed for the helm, and I slid into the navigator's position just in front and to the right of the Captain's chair. It had been awhile since I'd filled in here.

"Request identification," the Captain ordered.

"Yes sir." Mr. Yanendale spoke into his headset. "This is *Surveyor*, please identify."

I looked over my shoulder and watched his face. A broad grin spread over it, and he took off the headset and said, "On speakers, Captain."

"What..."

A voice I knew better than I knew my own came over the speakers. "Repeat, this is *Alacrity I*, requesting permission to lock on."

I couldn't resist a squeal of delight. The *Alacrity I* hadn't been around for almost a year.

The Captain pressed the intercom button on his chair. "You're free to come and go as you please, as I'm sure you know, sir."

"I thought as much," the voice returned. "Approaching. Don't tell Uncle—I want to surprise him."

The Captain looked at me, and I nodded.

"Copy that, *Alacrity I*." He switched off his intercom and began to give orders. "Propulsion to zero, Mr. Guilders."

"Aye, sir."

"Mr. Ralston, standby to lock off life support systems in airlock one."

"Life support systems standing by."

The Captain spoke into his wristcom. "Commander Howitz, send a mate to operate moorings at port peripheral access one."

"Aye sir," came a gravelly voice from the com.

"Engage airlock one, Mr. Ralston."

"Airlock one, engaged, sir."

"*Alacrity I* is clear to moor," the Captain directed.

Mr. Yanendale nodded and relayed the message.

"Track *Alacrity I* on scopes, Mr. Whales."

"Yes sir."

I smiled at Guilders. "So are you two going to have it out this time?"

His bushy eyebrows didn't move as he answered pragmatically, "If he doesn't challenge me, I won't challenge him."

"And if he does?"

Instead of answering, he turned his attention to the approaching speeder, which had just switched from warp speed to propulsion, and now did a daring three hundred and sixty degree flip as it approached.

I smiled in pure delight, and the Captain shook his head. "The devil. He knows we're watching him."

Finally, after a few more little showy maneuvers, the

speeder zoomed past the port window, and a moment later, the voice came again over the speakers. "The Eagle has Crashed."

"Copy that, *Alacrity I*."

I laughed and stood up, straightening my jacket and trying to straighten my face as I turned towards the Captain. "Request permission to welcome guest aboard, sir."

Shaking his head at me with an exaggerated sigh, the Captain said, "Permission granted," in an amused tone. Then to Mr. Ralston, "Seal and disengage airlock one. Guilders, tie navigation into the helm until Andi gets back."

"Aye, Captain."

Gesturing towards the door, the Captain smiled at me. That was the only encouragement I needed to rush off the bridge and into the elevator. "C-Deck," I indicated, and was moved downwards. From the elevator, I hurried down the corridor until I reached the entrance to airlock one. It was still closed, and I leaned forward as I waited for it to slide open.

When it did, I beheld thirty-two year old, dark-haired, grinning Eagle Crash, with his arms crossed over his chest in a jaunty attitude. His dark leather jacket and deep red pants and shirt only added to the impression he immediately gave anyone who saw him: adventurer.

"Greetings, cousin," were his first words as he stepped from the chamber. I rushed to embrace him.

"Crash, so good to see you again!"

He good-naturedly put his arm around my shoulders. "Didn't tell Uncle, did you?"

"No. I was on the bridge when you arrived. I heard you."

"Ah, then you saw my little stunts?"

"You know I did!" I laughed. "How do you want to break the news to the Doctor?"

"Come, come, Andi, don't talk about it as if we were going to a funeral. Don't you think my dear uncle will be thrilled to see me?" He offered me his arm.

Laughing, I took it, and we started towards sickbay.

"Thrilled may be a slight overstatement." I lowered my voice. "But he will be glad to see you. Even if he doesn't show it."

"Oh, don't worry. I've known the old fellow longer than you have, I know his ups and downs like nobody else. But tell me how things have been around the old *Surveyor.*"

I began to relate our adventures since he'd last visited. Crash—nobody ever called him Eagle—was like the older brother I'd always wished for. Though I had only been six, I remembered when the Doctor sat me down and told me that his younger sister had died, his sister, whom I had never met but had heard of many times. He'd told me about my cousin, Eagle, who was eighteen years old and would be staying with us while he continued his training as a space pilot.

Four years Crash had stayed with us, and four years didn't seem long at all with him around. Despite the difference in our ages, and the fact that I wasn't even related to him, he took an immediate interest in me, and involved me in many of his adventures. Some were good memories; like the time he snuck me into one of his pilot academy classes when I was seven, and let me fly the simulator. Others were not so good, like when the Doctor had caught us draining the lox out of the rocket base fuel tanks. And then there were some that involved a mixture of feelings, like the time he'd taken the Doctor and I on our first space flight. I'd loved it, but the Doctor, to say the least, had *not*, and made it thoroughly clear that he would never again enter a craft that Crash piloted if his life depended on it.

In spite of all this, I'd seen the wistfulness behind the Doctor's eyes lately whenever we spoke of his nephew. Even a hint of worry—it had been so long since we'd heard from him. But now he was here, and all was well. I couldn't wait to see the look on the Doctor's face when his eyes fell on the sturdy form beside me.

I talked on as we hurried in and out of the elevator and down the halls, and we came in sight of the last bend before sickbay so quickly that I didn't have time to ask him what he'd been up to. Pulling me against the wall, he whispered, "Go on in and talk to him."

"What do you want me to say?" I giggled.

"Anything that doesn't have to do with me. I'll take care of the rest, now scoot!"

Pushing me out, he winked, and slipped back into his corner. I straightened my jacket, cleared my throat, and walked towards sickbay. "Doctor?

He came out of the room, rubbing a glob of sanitizer between his hands. "What is it, Andi? I'm busy."

"I—wanted to show you something," I grinned.

"What?" he asked, with some impatience.

I waited for Crash to come bouncing out, but I heard nothing. I waited for a moment. Still nothing.

"Well?" He tapped his foot.

"I just... thought you might want to see something," I stammered, turning to look over my shoulder. How long did he expect me to stall?

"Yes, I would like to see something, I'd like to see you either in there helping me, or up on the bridge helping Captain Trent like he asked you to."

I turned back. "But... I really need to show you something."

"Well then, show me." The irritation in his voice was growing.

I turned back to look over my shoulder again, hoping desperately that Crash would show himself. "Well..."

"Why do you keep turning your head like that? Is someone back there?" Moving past me, he peered around the corner. "Have you gone crazy?"

I watched him, puzzled. "No, I just..."

As he turned back to face me, I saw surprise light up his eyes, then a second of disbelief, followed by another of gladness, and then he managed to compose himself into a half-affectionate, half-stern expression resembling a smile. I didn't need to ask who was behind me, although how he had gotten there, I had no idea at first. After thinking it over for a moment, I realized that Crash had ducked into the sanitation room from the hall and then walked through into sickbay, coming out behind me.

"Well, Mr. Crash." He advanced and shook the young man's hand. Crash winked at me and laughed, and I felt that he was somehow both laughing with me and laughing at me. "How is it that no one mentioned that you were here?"

"The how of it is, Uncle, that I asked them not to. I wanted to surprise you. You were surprised, weren't you?"

"You scoundrel, you know I was. Why I allow myself to be taken in by all your schemes is beyond me, I'll tell you that much."

I grabbed the Doctor's arm happily. "Isn't it good to see Crash again, Doctor?

He looked at Crash's handsome, friendly, and slightly impish face and had to say, "Yes I suppose it is." But in an instant his tone changed, and he grunted, "What business had you to stay away for so long?"

Crash sobered down. "It's not why I stayed away that's important right now; it's why I came back when I did."

His tone was unusually serious, and the Doctor looked even more confused than I felt. He peered at Crash. "What in blazes are you talking about?"

"Did you hear about Doctor Holmes?"

I watched as the Doctor's face registered curiosity mingled with worry. "I haven't heard from him in months. Is something wrong?"

Crash hesitated for a moment, then spoke solemnly.

"He died last month."

CHAPTER III

"Died?" I whispered, surprised. The Doctor laid an arm across my shoulders. I had known Doctor Holmes on Earth—he had been the Doctor's employer during his medical residency, and the two had remained good friends afterward. I remembered him as a kind, grandfatherly gentleman who always took an interest in me and Crash.

Now, the Doctor's brows furrowed and he bit his lower lip, which I understood to indicate sorrow, but he only said, "What does that have to do with you coming here?"

Shaking his head, Crash gave an odd smile. "I'm not quite sure myself. But I need to talk to you."

He didn't say "in private," but I understood anyway. The Doctor frowned. "I can't talk right now. I have a patient in there that needs tending. Tonight."

Crash nodded, and the men grasped hands again. Abruptly, the Doctor turned to me. "All right, you've had your fun. Now go do your job."

"Yes sir." I was looking forward to being present at the confrontation between the mischievous, daring Crash and the practical, cautious Guilders, which was always a source of amusement.

"Talk to you later, my boy," said the Doctor brusquely, and he hurried back into sickbay.

I beamed at Crash. "He must be even more glad to see you than I thought. He hasn't called you 'my boy' since you left on the *Alacrity I* the first time."

"Yes." There was an absent look in his eyes for a moment that puzzled me, but in an instant it was gone, and a look of fun flashed in its place. "Going up to see the Captain and Guilders, are we?"

"Don't be surprised if Guilders doesn't jump for joy when he sees you."

"Hmm, on second thought, we should go visit Almira first. She'll give me a hug and call me 'honey' and get me cheered up to go see the grumps upstairs."

"No," I chuckled, "you've already gone against regulations by visiting the Doctor before reporting to the Captain."

"Now Andi, have you ever known me to follow regulations?"

"No time like the present."

His only answer was a good-natured laugh. With an exaggerated bow, and a "Lead the way, m'lady," he followed me up to the bridge.

When we reached it, Crash stepped out in his usual cocky manner and announced, "Crash on the bridge, sir."

The Captain swiveled his chair around. "So I see. It took you long enough to get up here." He pretended to disapprove, but I could tell that he was just as pleased as any of us to see Crash again. Guilders, however, didn't even turn around.

"Yes, Trent, good to see you too." In five steps he was beside the chair and was wringing the Captain's hand. Turning to wink at me, he looked in Guilders' direction. I giggled as I slid into the navigator's seat again. Loudly, he said, "I can see by the way Guilders flew up to greet me that he's glad I'm here."

The Captain's eyes twinkled.

Guilders said in a calm voice, "Mr. Crash, I can see you haven't changed in the last year."

Crash knelt beside the helmsman on one knee and wrapped an arm affectionately around his neck. "Yes, I'm happy to say you're right. You haven't changed either—just as spontaneous and joyful as ever."

Without losing his composure, Guilders pried the pilot's arm from his neck. "I'm thankful to say you're right."

I took pity on the older man. "Crash, hadn't you better go say hello to Almira?"

"Woah, not so fast." Standing up, Crash faced the Captain with a business look on his face. "What's your heading, and why are you going through uncharted sectors?"

"Alpha fifty-four-thirty-three. We had some apparent reactions to our probes there, so we're on our way to have a look. This is the shortest route, and you know the owner doesn't like to be kept waiting. We're already having trouble with one of the smaller thrusters."

"Remind me, this is the hundredth time you've had so-called 'reactions'?"

I was afraid the Captain might launch into a long discussion on the subject of the probability of life on other planets, but he only laughed good-naturedly and said, "Only the twenty-third, Mr. Crash, and don't be the skeptic, I have enough of that with your uncle."

"I am my uncle's nephew, Captain."

"Forgive me, I didn't know. Spare me the debate, I've had my fill for today."

"You talked to Uncle about it?"

"You might say he talked to me about it."

"I thought as much." Crash winked at me again. "One of these days, you'll give up, and you'll have to admit we're right."

The Captain would have retaliated if it weren't for the interruption of the science exec at that moment. "Obstruction ahead, Captain."

"Element scan, Mr. Whales."

"Aye sir."

"Propulsion 10, Mr. Guilders."

"Adjusting to IPP 10, sir."

"We'll discuss this later, Mr. Crash," the Captain took the time to say, then he turned back to the fore. "Mr. Guilders, prepare to maneuver around the object."

Guilders switched control from navigation to the helm, and I relaxed somewhat. Navigation was not my favorite task.

"We're still out of range of the comm towers?" the Captain clarified.

"Yes sir. We won't be in range again for another..." Mr. Yanendale checked his computer. "Five sectors."

Five sectors. That was—somewhere around 5000 light years. A long time to go without being able to communicate with Earth or any distant ships.

"Andi, no records for this area in the database?"

I leaned forward and scanned the records upon which navigation depended. "No sir, we just passed the last officially charted sector in this direction."

The Captain leaned back in his chair and muttered an oath. "We should have gotten records from the *Comet III* before we went out of range."

"Should we turn back, sir?" Guilders asked.

"No. Let's see just what it is first."

Crash stepped to the Captain's side and said, "Request permission to operate the helm, sir."

I groaned inwardly. Not again. Glancing at Guilders, I watched in vain for a change of expression.

The Captain seemed to hesitate, but finally said, "Mr. Guilders is doing a sufficient job, Mr. Crash. I don't see the need..."

"But I do. If we're approaching a nebula or an asteroid belt, you're going to need someone with experience."

"Mr. Crash, our helmsman has had ample experience."

"But not in this area. If I am correct, sir, the *Surveyor* has never ventured beyond sector forty-eight-ten in this direction."

"You are correct, nevertheless, I do not see the need to change helm control at this time."

"But Captain..."

"Mr. Crash, I believe the answer I gave you was no." The Captain raised his voice in irritation. "If that is not sufficiently clear..."

"Four minutes to impact," came the science exec's voice. "Instruments aren't finished registering."

"Slow to propulsion five."

"Aye sir."

"Power up the navicomputer, Andi, and plot a course to the edge of this sector."

"Yes sir." I sat up and began to follow his command. The navicomputer always took some time to compute a safe course, so I was surprised when, moments after I'd told it to begin plotting, it beeped at me.

I read the error message from the panel aloud. "Error, computation impossible. Cluster approaching, mark 104.57."

The Captain frowned. "Cluster?"

"Confirmed," spoke up Mr. Whales. "Space trash ahead, various elements."

"Anything dangerous?" the Captain asked.

"No sir. But it's large. At least ninety astronomical units."

"Ninety? Are you sure?"

"Cluster visible," announced Guilders, who hadn't spoken during the discussion about helm control.

I looked up and watched as the massive field of trash came into view. Asteroids mainly, at least that's all I could pick out. We were still a few thousand kilometers away from it and already it spanned the entire fore window.

The Captain paused for half a second before ordering "Propulsion to one, Mr. Guilders."

I watched as the rapid approach of the cluster slowed to a crawl, wondering what the Captain's decision would be. If the cluster were stable—an asteroid belt or a small system—then it would have only taken a few minutes, even seconds, to go around it at almost any warp factor. But the instability of the trash made it more difficult. Warp was dangerous, because one of the rocks might jump out in front of us, resulting in a crash that would probably be fatal. Using plasma propulsion, however, would take a couple of hours, and we were on a tighter schedule than usual, with one thruster out of commission. The owner of the *Surveyor* was not a particularly patient man, and I knew that Captain Trent's punctuality was one thing that had kept him in command for so many years.

I turned to look at his face as he pondered. He took so long that Guilders dared prompt, "Parabolic course, Captain?"

No one except Guilders or the Doctor would have been allowed such a liberty. The Captain sighed. "I don't suppose it's safe to go through?"

"No sir," Guilders answered.

"Trent," Crash broke in, "I've gone through trash fields safely before."

There was a silence on the bridge for a few seconds. Then the Captain shook his head. "No. We'll go around. IPP ten, Mr. Guilders, and keep a sharp eye. Andi, be ready to plot course to the next sector once we're on the other side."

"Yes sir." I'd already set the destination, so there was nothing more I could do until Guilders had worked his maneuvering magic.

"Wait!"

Crash again. I frowned, wondering at his persistence. Did he not trust Guilders? Or was he just trying to prove himself?

"Mr. Crash..."

"I can take us around at warp 8."

There was another momentary pause. The Captain stared. Guilders didn't turn around, didn't twitch an eyebrow—nothing.

Crash was an exceptional pilot. No one could dispute that. But Guilders had years more experience. I bit my lip.

"Stability level of the field, Mr. Whales?" the Captain requested.

"Calculating... level two, sir."

Level two. That was extremely unstable.

If he hesitated too long, it would be moot. He cleared his throat and finally said, "Very well, Mr. Crash."

I felt for Guilders as he stood up and stepped aside. His face showed no anger or frustration, but I knew he must be hurt by the decision. It wasn't my place to remark, however, so I kept silent and turned my face towards the fore.

Crash slid deftly into the chair and laid his hands on the controls with a smile. Taking the control column with one hand, he reached to adjust the warp slider to eight.

I gripped the navigation panel and tensed. Crash was good, but—something didn't feel right. Cocky as he was, there was some kind of subtext to his insistence on taking the helm that I couldn't put my finger on. For some reason, he was out to prove himself.

Smoothly, the ship accelerated, through the earlier warp levels and up to warp eight. The massive trash cluster moved to the starboard window, and I barely felt the motion as Crash maneuvered us around it.

I realized I had been holding my breath and I let it out softly as we moved by the trash. Sometimes a rock whizzed so close by the window that I winced a bit, but the path ahead stayed clear.

Twice, a stray asteroid flew too close to us, and the ship swung away, but we were moving so quickly that the danger was over almost before I'd noticed it. A thick silence and suspense hung over the bridge, and I stole a sidelong glance at Guilders. His eyes were focused on the fore window, and he didn't move.

"Halfway there," Mr. Whales announced from the science station.

"Good…" the Captain began, but at that moment a rock the size of the bridge swerved in front of us.

I yelled "Look out!" as Crash pummeled controls, but it was too late, and the asteroid slammed into the *Surveyor*'s main body.

CHAPTER IV

The ship jolted violently, knocking everyone out of their seats. My head hit the back of my chair and I fell to the floor, landing with my shoulder to the ground. At first I wasn't hurt, only shaken. Smoke came from somewhere on my right, and a confused mass of voices rose around me as everyone tried to get back to their stations. Above them all, the Captain's steely voice rose, trying to keep everyone calm and organized. But before I had time to take any of this in, a searing pain shot through my right knee.

It was unlike any pain I'd ever known. Burning, unbearable pain as if my kneecap were red hot. Agony exploded in my leg, causing me to scream and clutch at my knee with both hands. Just seconds after the first pain, another spasm wrenched through my leg and I crumpled, crying with the intense misery.

In a second, Guilders was at my side. He laid his hand on my shoulder and tried to talk to me, but I couldn't focus on what he was saying.

The Doctor's voice, more worried than I'd heard it in a long time, came from my wristcom, breaking through the fog of pain that enshrouded my mind. "Andi? Andi, where are you?"

I couldn't answer, as another spasm grabbed my knee. Just when I didn't think I could stand the intensity of the pain another second, it died off suddenly, leaving a throbbing heat.

Guilders grabbed my wrist and spoke into the com. "Gerard, something's wrong with her."

"Guilders!" The Captain's voice rose out of the confusion.

"Take the helm."

At the same time a voice struggled from my wristcom. "I'll be right there."

I heard shouting; Crash shouting, the Captain shouting back, but the words wouldn't come into focus. With a hurried, soft touch on my shoulder, Guilders stood up and walked away. I opened my eyes and saw the Captain yank Crash from the helm and pull back the warp slider, and then step back to allow Guilders to work the panel.

I closed my eyes again and began crying, still clutching my knee. I didn't dare take my hands away—I was afraid the pain would come back. I felt like a little child.

The commotion around me just sounded like a solid buzz, and I smelled smoke from somewhere on my right. I was still sobbing when a shaking hand was laid on my head.

I looked up into Crash's eyes. They held a mix of anger and fear, and his voice trembled as he asked, "What's wrong?"

"Don't let it come back," I whimpered.

He stood up and bent down to lift me. I was still gripping my knee and I shut my eyes tight again, but I felt his arms close around me and then I had a sensation of being carried along. Confused voices kept up the chaos, and after a moment I heard a door slide open and then a hand was laid on my forehead.

"Andi?"

I opened my eyes to see the Doctor standing there, with such a lovingly concerned face it made me want to cry all over again.

"Dad... it's my knee..." I began. "Dad, I..."

He grasped my hand just as everything turned to black.

* * *

"That's all?" were the first words I heard when I regained consciousness. They seemed far away and somehow vague, but I knew it was the Doctor's voice. "And that sent you up here like the

Devil was at your back?"

"That was all I heard from him." Crash's voice. "It was Leeke's departure that worried me. I think it's connected somehow."

"But what would they want with an old country doctor?"

"I don't know. But he said to warn you."

There was a silence, and footsteps echoed through the room. I realized I'd been brought into my quarters, and was now laying on my bed. A hand rested on my shoulder. "How is she?"

"She seems fine." The Doctor's voice held a hint of confusion. "Crash, you..."

I opened my eyes and looked up at the two men. "Dad? What happened?" I felt normal now, although there was a slight numbness in my knee.

Instead of answering, he asked me an abrupt question. "Andi, did you hit your knee when you fell?"

"No sir. I fell on my shoulder. That knee wasn't anywhere near the floor." I was a little annoyed with myself for not knowing what the problem was. I thought the Doctor had taught me everything about medicine and the human body, but my experience on the bridge didn't fit in with any kind of ailment or injury I'd ever heard of. I was well up on prosthetic complications, especially kneecap replacements, and I had never heard of anything remotely like that.

"I don't know, sweetheart." The Doctor's voice was so gentle it almost scared me. And he hadn't called me sweetheart since my sixteenth birthday.

I looked at Crash, who was knitting his brows and chewing on his lower lip. "What was that all about?"

He had the audacity to stare at me as if he didn't know what I was talking about. "What was *what* all about?"

"Your performance on the bridge."

He flushed, and looked angry. "I've taken the *Alacrity* through that exact cluster a dozen..."

"Starships aren't the same as speeders, Crash. You should

have let Guilders alone."

"Don't tell me what to do!"

"Crash," said the Doctor with firmness definite enough to silence even Crash. "Ask Almira to send down some soup."

"See you later, Andi."

As my cousin turned to leave the room, I called out, "I think you could at least apologize."

He stopped but didn't turn around. "I didn't mean for you to get hurt."

"I meant to Guilders."

Crash stiffened and hurried out.

"All right, tell me what exactly happened up there." The Doctor pulled a chair up next to where I lay.

I recounted the whole story, from the greeting between Crash, the Captain, and Guilders, to the first appearance of the cluster, to the jolt that had brought on the strange, intense knee pains. The Doctor kept quiet throughout, but when I finished, he took my hand in his and said, "If it happens again, you have to page me right away. And be sure to tell me immediately if you discover any other—symptoms."

"You have no idea what could have caused this?" I asked again. I knew he'd already said he didn't know, but that just didn't seem possible.

"It was the leg with your implant, right?"

I nodded.

"But you've never felt anything there before?"

"Maybe a couple little twinges, but *nothing* like this."

He tilted his head a little to one side. "I'm going to look up the symptom. But I've never encountered anything like this out of the blue."

I sighed. I hadn't either. But then, I wasn't as experienced as a real doctor, I'd just done some nursing and some assistant-level treatments.

He let go of my hand. "If I find out anything, I promise that you'll be the first to know."

Trying to smile, I prepared to get up, but he laid a restraining hand on my shoulder. "No, I want you to get some rest."

He started to stand, but I found I didn't want him to leave. I rifled my brain for a topic to keep him there. "Dad?"

He paused. "Yes?"

"I'm sorry about Doctor Holmes."

He smiled sadly, the professionalism melting away into an unusually empathetic attitude. "You remember him?"

"Yes sir."

"He was a good man. I'm sorry I couldn't keep up with him more in the last few years."

"How old were you when you started working for him?"

He considered for an instant, fingering his chin before he answered. "Twenty-nine. Still just a kid."

I tried to imagine him at twenty-nine, but couldn't get past his gray hair. I pictured a small version of himself with glasses—I knew he used to wear glasses—showing up at Doctor Holmes's door in sneakers and a tee-shirt. I giggled.

He frowned at me. "What's so funny about being twenty-nine?"

"Nothing. I wonder what Doctor Holmes has to do with Crash coming back?"

He licked his lips and looked at me as if trying to decide something. At last he said, "Crash is going to talk to me more later, but apparently he told Crash to warn me."

CHAPTER V

This wasn't what I'd been expecting at all. I sat up and stared at him, wide-eyed. "Warn you? About what?"

Shaking his head, he stood up. "We don't know. He called Crash from the hospital just before he died, and Crash says he didn't sound lucid. But he said Crash had to warn me."

I hesitated, then laid back down. "Do you think—well, maybe he didn't know what he was talking about? If he had some kind of dementia... what did he die of?"

"To the second question, Crash asked his doctor, and they don't know. It was some kind of insanity, but they could never pin down a source. He was dead less than a week after they'd brought him in. As for the first question—that's what I said. I have more respect for Emmett—Doctor Holmes—than almost anybody else I know, but he could definitely have been demented."

He paused here, and looked at me for a second. Then he went on. "But Crash says that he got a little worried because right after Emmett told him that, some scientists left Earth and headed this way. Some scientists he doesn't like."

Doctor Holmes warned Crash, and then some scientists that Crash didn't like left Earth. That didn't sound all that suspicious to me, especially since there were a lot of people my cousin decided not to like, and not always for good reasons.

A thought hit me. "You don't think that's the Howitzes, do you?"

The Doctor shook his head. "Impossible. They've been here for almost a month, and these men left just two weeks ago."

He shrugged and stood up. "It could be nothing. It's *probably* nothing."

"Do you have to go?" I begged. I didn't understand why I wanted him there so intensely, unless it was just the lingering memory of that terrible pain on the bridge.

"I need to check in on sickbay, but I'll come back down here to make out my records if you want."

That wasn't entirely what I wanted. I'd far rather he stay close to me—talk to me, sit with me. But I knew that was selfish, and he had struggled the past few weeks with finding time to make out his medical records.

"Thanks," I said.

"I'll be back soon." Turning, he left the room.

I tried to relax, listening to the soft whirring of the life support systems that always lulled me to sleep. My thoughts drifted to the puzzling, frightening incident on the bridge, and I began to ponder Crash's actions again. He was angry at the Captain and Guilders now, I knew, and wouldn't speak to them for several days at least—or however long he stayed on board, whichever came first. He probably wouldn't stay long. He never did.

Guilders would act like nothing had happened, in his usual stoic way. The Captain would be frustrated, but as long as Crash caused no more trouble, he'd keep his temper.

I remembered well the first time Crash had visited us on the *Surveyor*, the first confrontation between himself and our helmsman. Crash had challenged him to a maneuvering contest through the "hazard zone"—I hadn't known what that was at the time, but later Guilders explained to me that it was a network, almost a maze of trash pockets, so confusing that the most seasoned pilots were often lost there. Crash had been twenty-seven at the time, and even more cocky than he was now, and hadn't taken his loss very well—yes of course Guilders had beaten him. What did he expect? Guilders had been maneuvering since before Crash was born.

Since then, it had been one big contest after another with the two of them. At least through the years Crash had come to have genuine respect for Guilders, but even so, he got angry with him frequently. The two of them just had such different outlooks—not only with regard to piloting, but life in general. How Guilders felt about Crash was unsure, but it was my opinion that he merely tolerated him.

The Captain was easily frustrated with Crash as well, and was significantly more outspoken about it than Guilders. However, he had an open respect for the younger man's abilities, and in fits of admiration had declared that Crash would be an asset to the crew. Fortunately, Crash never accepted. We all knew that with him on the crew for any extended period of time, the Captain would be driven mad. Crash was his own authority, and had never been one to bow to anyone's superiority in any area.

The door slid open as I concluded these thoughts, and I half sat up, then recognized the Doctor with a smile.

"Everything fine up there, Doctor?"

He nodded, and I noticed a large record pad tucked under his arm. I stifled a sigh. It *was* a good opportunity for him to get his work done. Usually I didn't mind, but—I shuddered. I wanted someone to talk to, and who better than my dear Doctor?

Settling himself in the chair across the room, he turned on the pad and began making out his reports.

I fidgeted for a few minutes, wishing I could get up and do something. I wasn't used to inactivity. The Doctor had said I needed rest, though. Perhaps I could read?

My thoughts were interrupted by a beep at the door. "Come in," I called.

The door slid open, and young Lieutenant August Howitz walked in, balancing a covered metal tray in his hands.

The Doctor looked up from his work and frowned. He laid the pad down and stared at the newcomer.

August looked back and forth between me and the Doctor with slight embarrassment. "The cook needed someone to bring up your dinner," he explained, "and the Captain chose me."

The Doctor raised his eyebrows, and I sighed. I did wish the Captain would give up his matchmaking on my account. But then, knowing it wasn't the Lieutenant's fault, and not wanting to make him feel bad, I smiled. "Thank you. I am getting hungry." I reached for the tray, glad at least that the Doctor was there. I had a definite feeling that he wouldn't have liked me to be alone with the young man.

"Well," said the Doctor. "You've done your duty, Lieutenant."

The lieutenant flushed. "He told me to stay and wait for the dishes, so the cook wouldn't have to bother with them."

I glanced over at the Doctor, who frowned again. I couldn't help smiling—I foresaw a decided talk between him and Captain Trent in the near future.

"I suppose," the Doctor said at last, "you have to do what the Captain orders."

August nodded. "I'm sorry, sir..."

The Doctor gestured to the chair that I usually occupied. "Have a seat, boy."

Looking more awkward than ever, the young man sat down. I knew the Doctor meant to be kind, and I tried to straighten out the situation.

"I beg you, when you see the Captain again, tell him from me he needn't worry about my situation any more... I'm quite happy as I am."

His relieved nod was almost amusing. "I'll tell him."

There was a moment of silence, then the Doctor asked him, "Are you feeling better?"

"Much better, thank you, Doctor," he said. Then with a moment of hesitation, he turned to me. "And you, Miss Andi—I heard you had an accident?"

"I'm feeling fine now, thank you." I finished my soup and began to nibble the bread. "Where were you when we hit the asteroid?"

"I was actually asleep in our quarters. The crash woke me, and I had to get up and take care of some of my father's things... He has a lot of tools and machinery in there, and they got knocked around a lot."

"What does your father do?" he asked.

"Here he's the first engineer. On Earth he was—an inventor."

"Andi's an inventor," the Doctor said.

August's eyes widened. "Really?"

I smiled fondly, but shook my head. "Just a hobby. I don't do much with it." I paused to take a drink. "What has your dad invented?"

He shrugged. "He doesn't really make things for the general public. Special computers and service technology, that kind of thing."

"And what about you?" the Doctor probed.

August frowned. "I'm a navigator. I've done a little electrical engineering, but nothing like him."

"Do you always work together?" I asked, swallowing the last bite of bread, and watching as he stood up.

"No." He walked over and took the tray from me. "After I graduated I went to space alone—I was a navigator on the *Beagle*. He came and picked me up about a month ago."

"Why?" I asked.

"He'd heard that your engineer was on extended leave for his honeymoon and decided to take the position, and he heard that your navigator had died as well. I guess he just thought I'd be good for the position."

The Lieutenant shifted the tray to a more comfortable position as he stood talking, and I thought I detected a wistfulness in his voice, as if he *hoped* his father thought he'd be good for the position, but rather doubted it.

The door slid open as he finished, and Crash strode in. "Had your dinner And... Well, who's this?"

August turned to face him. "Lieutenant Howitz, navigator,

sir."

"I don't remember seeing you on the bridge."

"He was resting, Crash," I explained. "Health problems. Lieutenant, this is my cousin, Eagle Crash."

August's eyes widened, and he balanced the tray on his arm, then carefully put out his hand to shake Crash's. "A pleasure, sir." He turned back to me. "Eagle Crash is your cousin?"

Crash grinned, as he always did when any reference was made to his fame. "She's lucky that way."

His grin faded when August turned to face him again, and he peered at the pale face and dark eyes for a moment. "Have I met you somewhere?"

"No sir, I'm sure I would remember meeting you."

Crash straightened up. "What did you say your name was again?"

"Howitz, August Howitz."

"Austrian, are you?"

"I grew up there, sir, but I am a United States citizen by birth."

"I see. Well, you don't have to 'sir' me."

"Yes sir. I mean no sir. I mean..." August flushed, and I stifled a giggle. He stood up a bit straighter and shifted the tray to a more comfortable position. "I suppose I should be taking this down to the galley."

"Yes, I suppose you should."

The Lieutenant turned and nodded at me and the Doctor, then hurried out, obviously intimidated by Crash's commanding, confident manner, as well as his reputation.

The Doctor cleared his throat and picked up his pad. "If you're going to be up here for a minute, I'm going to go have some dinner myself."

"When can I get up?" I asked.

He looked at me and thought about it. Then he came to a conclusion. "Right now, I'd like you to keep resting for tonight. When I come back up, we can talk about you getting up in the morning."

"Yes sir."

He left the room, and I watched with a slight sigh as the door closed behind him.

I already missed work, missed eating in the big mess hall with everyone else, missed bantering with the Doctor throughout the afternoon.

I wanted things to go back to normal.

CHAPTER VI

Crash walked forward a few steps. "Are you still mad at me?"

"I wasn't mad at you. I just don't like you to argue with them."

"'Them?'"

"The Captain and Guilders."

He held up his hand. "Please, I just ate."

"Crash, that's not funny! Don't talk about them like that. It was *your* fault, you know. The Captain trusted you, and..."

"It wasn't my fault!" he protested. "If I'd been in the *Alacrity I*, I could have..."

"But this wasn't the *Alacrity I*, it was a starship. Why couldn't you just trust Guilders?"

In his usual cavalier manner, his answer was to change the subject. "Who was that fellow who was in here just now?"

I sighed. "He told you. Lieutenant Howitz, the navigator."

"You know him?" He pulled a chair closer to me and hung his jacket over the back.

"I just met him today. I treated him in sickbay this morning, and then he and his dad were with the Captain during lunch..."

"His dad?" Crash had seated himself in the chair, and now he sat upright. "His father is on board, too?"

I was puzzled by this line of questioning. "Why are you asking me all this? Do you know him?"

"I don't know." He sat back and threw his arm across the back of the chair. "He reminded me of someone I knew when I was a little kid."

"Is that the person you told the Doctor had left Earth?"

"Oh, so he told you about that?" He stood up and started to pace. "No, he's not the person who left Earth. And *his* name isn't Howitz—neither of them are named Howitz. It's Leeke, and his assistant, Mars. But I haven't seen them here." He sat down again and tried to relax. "What do you know about this Howitz?"

"August... his name's August. He and his dad have been on the ship a month, and his dad is the first engineer. He suffers from orthostatic hypotension..."

"Woah, woah, don't be giving me doctor's talk, Andi. You know I don't like it."

"Well you know I don't like you arguing with the Captain and Guilders."

"That's different."

"Why is it different?"

"Because I'm older than you."

I was about to give some indignant reply, but he intercepted it.

"I don't think you understand, Andi. I'm sorry you got hurt, but part of being an adventurer is to take risks. Guilders isn't willing to do that, and that's why he'll never grow as a pilot. He's afraid."

This almost made sense—but it wasn't right. First of all, Guilders never seemed afraid to me. Secondly—

"Don't you think it's a little presumptuous for you to say Guilders won't grow? He's had so much more experience than you..." I wanted to add, "and you're the one who crashed us, not him," but I didn't.

He smiled patiently. "That's the point. He *is* more experienced than me. By virtue of the fact that he was in space when I was in diapers, I know that. But which one of us is *better*?"

He expected me to say him. It was logical. He was a famous pilot, with clients lining up for his services. He'd done things no one had done in the history of space travel until he came along. He'd flown jobs for governments, scientists, and lots of jobs he couldn't even tell us about.

Guilders, on the other hand, had just been a quiet helmsman on a chartered exploration vessel for thirty years.

"The Doctor trusts Guilders..." I began.

"Of course. I trust him—usually. But in the face of an emergency, which one of us is willing to step out do what needs to be done, regardless of consequences?"

I was confused. Crash was, that was true. But didn't he have a lot more accidents than Guilders? Was that true courage, or just rashness?

I shook my head but didn't answer. After an awkward silence, a rarity between the two of us, I asked, "How long until we reach Alpha fifty-four-thirty-three?"

"Too long for my taste. That asteroid damaged the attitude control system, and your beloved Guilders is creeping at a snail's pace until it's repaired. It should take a couple days to get it up and running again."

"The Captain's not happy, is he?"

"Nope, not one bit. But then, what else is new?"

"Crash, please..."

"Sorry, And. I forgot, no captain or helmsman bashing allowed."

I didn't feel like talking to him anymore. "Goodnight, Crash."

He whistled, and stood up. "That's a subtle hint. Well, goodnight, cousin. See you tomorrow."

Picking up his jacket and throwing it over his shoulder, he left.

Sitting up after the door closed behind him, I pulled up my skirt to take a look at my knee. There was no sign of anything wrong, not even the slightest degree of redness.

With a sigh, I realized how late it was getting, and thought I should get to bed. I was tired, emotionally and physically, and sleep sounded attractive just then. I stood up carefully, wary of putting pressure on the knee. It felt a little numb as I walked to the door to lock it, but otherwise normal. I then proceeded to dress for bed.

After I'd thrown on a nightgown and brushed my teeth, I knelt beside the bed to pray. My thoughts wandered, however, slipping through the events of the day. Not just my knee pains, though that was enough to think about. Crash played a large part in my thoughts, as did August and his father. There was also Doctor Holmes's strange warning and the people that Crash didn't like who had left Earth.

I didn't like any of it. Things had been perfectly fine when I woke up that morning.

I jerked my thoughts back to my prayer again. *Lord, thank you for protecting the ship today. Thank you for—*for what? What had I been going to say? My thoughts were wandering again. Was the Doctor really in any danger? Could my knee have anything to do with Doctor Holmes? Surely not.

I snapped my thoughts back again. *Please protect us all, Lord. Don't let anything bad happen to us.* Don't let anything bad happen to us? How flat was that. But that was really all I wanted at the moment. *Keep us safe. Thanks. Goodnight.*

As I crawled under the covers, I felt unsatisfied somehow. I called to the lights to turn off, then snarled in the dark, pulling the blankets up under my chin. It was all Crash's fault, I decided. He'd brought us these silly suspicions and he'd made a mistake on the bridge. But now everything was fine, the malfunctions would be repaired soon, and in the meantime, I should relax.

Sleep came quickly, and I wasn't bothered by dreams, at least not that I could remember. When I drifted back to consciousness the next morning, I became aware of a beeping nearby.

I kept my eyes closed, not moving. The beeping went on, and I pulled the covers over my head.

It didn't stop, and I was forced to put the covers down and look around for the source.

My wristcom. I was being paged.

Gripping it clumsily off my nightstand, I answered the call. "Yes?"

"Andi, I'm leaving. I thought you'd want me to wake you up."

My brain buzzed tiredly as I tried to place the voice. Crash.

"Leaving?" I mumbled. "Where—are you going?"

"Get dressed and come to airlock one."

I laid down the com and dragged myself out of bed. Still half asleep, I went through the motions of pulling on my uniform and dragging a comb languidly through my hair. I was not a morning person—as opposed to Crash and the Doctor, both of whom could jump out of bed in the wee hours of the morning and be fully lucid immediately.

Forgetting to put my wristcom on, I stumbled out of the room and made my way somehow through the dim halls to airlock one. Dim lights—what time was it, anyway? It must be before six.

When I reached the airlock, it was open. Crash and the Doctor were inside, speaking soberly. I heard the Doctor say, "I don't know. I just met him."

"He's altogether too much like Sandison for my liking." Crash scowled as he said this. "I never did like him."

"You don't know that it is him."

Crash turned then and saw me, blinking sleepily in the entrance. "Where are you going?" I asked.

"They've bamboozled me into being a scout."

I was unaware that anyone could bamboozle him into anything. "A scout?"

The Doctor moved to my side and put an arm around my shoulders, shaking me slightly to wake me. "Trent and that new Commander decided it would be a good idea to send him ahead with Whales."

Whales... Mr. Whales was the scientist. "To test for life?"

"Yes."

I found myself wondering if Guilders had been involved in

the decision at all. "Kind of... sudden, isn't it?" I was still not entirely awake.

"Trent asked me about it last night," Crash explained. "But you were already asleep."

I wanted to protest that I'd been asleep when he called me, but I resisted. Besides, I knew I would have been mad if I'd awakened and found that he'd left without saying goodbye.

The Captain strode in, already shaved and uniformed, looking as fresh and energetic as if he'd been up and about for hours.

"How are preparations going, Mr. Crash?" he asked.

Mr. Whales appeared behind him, lugging a crate of equipment. Crash caught his eye and jerked his head towards the access of the *Alacrity I*. Whales nodded and began carrying his load towards the speeder.

"Almost done," Crash answered. "Should just be a couple minutes."

I was too sleepy for a moment to figure out just how the *Alacrity I* was going to get there before us. Then I remembered that speeders could travel at higher velocities than starships, because they were built for nothing but speed. The *Alacrity* could get there and back in half the time it would take the *Surveyor* to reach Alpha fifty-four-thirty-three—and not only because of the higher warp factors. Speeders could take more direct routs than larger ships, and there was one other thing. I struggled to recollect it.

The Captain helped me without meaning to. "I want you to employ warp as long as possible... If memory serves, the *Alacrity I* is a 4k speeder?"

Of course. How close a craft could get to an object without having to slow to propulsion. The *Surveyor* was closer to a 12k.

Crash's chest expanded with pride. "3k, sir."

"3k?" The Captain's eyes widened. "I've never even heard of a 3k."

"Excuse me, Trent, but you have. You've heard of the *Alacrity I*."

I giggled, and the Captain had to smile. "I suppose I shall have to concede that."

Crash's eyes went past the Captain, and he smiled. "She can actually get a little closer than that, but to be safe, I say 3k."

I turned to look and saw Guilders standing there. Suddenly, I understood, at least partially, why Crash had allowed himself to be talked into this.

"I don't think anyone would believe a 2k," Guilders commented, stepping in.

Crash sniffed, and turned away. "Are you ready Mr. Whales?"

Whales stuck his head out of the access. "I'm ready."

"Be careful," the Captain said. "You should be able to stay in contact with us the whole time."

"I think so." Crash approached me and the Doctor and looked at us with a smile. "I'll be back in a few days."

I nodded, and the Doctor laid a hand on Crash's shoulder, but said nothing.

Crash turned to me and opened his arms. I flew to them and hugged him tight, feeling a sudden pang of guilt for blaming my unrest on him.

"Stay out of trouble while I'm gone," he joked.

"I will," I assured, my voice muffled by his jacket.

He let me go, and with a last smile, disappeared into the *Alacrity I*'s access.

"Clear the airlock," a technician called through the intercom, and I reluctantly backed out and into the hall, watching the opening of Crash's speeder until the airlock entrance slid shut with a loud whoosh.

I felt a strong vibration as the speeder pulled free from her moorings, and zoomed out into open space.

I caught a glimpse of the *Alacrity* through the porthole as it raced away. It was a good idea to send him off, it would help us. It was a logical move for the Captain to make.

So why was a feeling of unease settling over me?

CHAPTER VII

I sighed as Guilders and the Captain retreated down the corridor, discussing the day's agenda. The Doctor squeezed my shoulders.

"Can I go to breakfast?" I asked. The lights came on as I said the word "go."

He raised an eyebrow. "Breakfast? At six in the morning?"

"Getting up early makes me hungry."

"All right. But it doesn't make me hungry, so I'm going to sickbay." He paused for a moment, and I turned to look at his face. I found hesitation there. "Meet me there at nine."

I stared. I went there every day. Something didn't sound right, though—"meet" him there? And why nine, why not just when I was ready, casually, like always?

"Is something wrong?" I asked.

"I—I don't know." He let go of my shoulders. "I want to test you for something."

Test me for something? For what?

"All right. Yes sir."

He walked away, and I watched his thin form shuffle off, feeling a little pain in my chest. I loved him so much. I didn't want anything to happen to him. Crash was just mistaken—the Doctor wasn't in any danger.

I loitered into the mess hall, knowing that the main breakfast would not be ready. Snack bar might not even be open yet. But if it wasn't, I could get myself something.

The large room was empty as I walked in, and I felt a

strange loneliness in the pit of my stomach. Then, as I trotted towards the galley, I saw a solitary form seated at the bar, in a waiting attitude.

All I could see from behind was that it was a large man, with dark, short brown hair. But when he heard my boot tap on the metal floor, he turned his head. Commander Howitz.

He smiled when he saw me. "Are you here to open the bar?" he asked.

"No," I smiled back, despite the fact that I didn't feel like smiling just then. "I don't actually work here. I was just hungry. But I can get you something if you like—Almira won't mind."

"Thank you," he said, his low, gravelly voice managing to unnerve me once again. "Where do you work, if not here?"

"Sickbay," I answered, slipping behind the counter. "I'm the second medical officer."

"Ah."

Was it just me, or was he uncomfortable around me, too? It was a fleeting impression, and the next moment he smiled a kind smile at me.

"I heard you had an accident on the bridge."

I flipped on the snack bar lights. "Yes. I hurt my knee, but we're not sure what caused it."

"'We'?"

"Doctor Lloyd—my father and I."

"Ah," he said again. He frowned, and peered at me, his small, black eyes seeming to take in every detail of me, almost hungrily.

I fidgeted, then entered my code into the temperature regulator. It beeped and unlocked, and I opened it. "What would you like to eat?"

"Andi?"

I turned to look at him and found him still staring at me.

"Yes?"

"Let me see your hand."

Hesitating, I closed the doors and stepped towards him. I

held out my hand slowly, and he didn't touch it, but looked closely at my palm.

He frowned more. "Have you ever been tested for Langham's Disease?"

Langham's Disease. I wracked my brain for details, but came up blank. "I don't think so—what is it?"

He looked up at my face, and I dropped my hand. "Langham's Disease is a disorder of the lymphatics. It's only been around for about thirty years, I don't think they know much about it yet. I'm not a doctor, remember, just an engineer. But I've seen it before. Your father's really never tested you for it?"

"No." I quelled the nervousness rising in me. "Is it serious?"

"Very. It's fatal. But I don't suppose you have it. I think it can only be developed during embryogenesis, or else transmitted to the mother during pregnancy. You've—" he hesitated "—never been pregnant?"

"No," I said, a little indignantly.

"Then if you had it, you would have died long ago." He shook his head. "Still, what I heard about your knee and what I saw just now..." he left his sentence unfinished.

"What did you see? And how would I know for sure?" I asked.

"I saw a slight swelling on your wrist. That usually means a fluid buildup, which is indicative of a lymphatic deficiency. Sudden, intense joint pains can occur in some cases." He seemed to anticipate my next question. "I had an employer whose wife was diagnosed once. He shared his research with me."

I was silent. I'd never heard of Langham's Disease—but then, he said it was rare, and little known about it. I studied my wrist. Was it a little swollen? I thought so.

He spoke again. "I'm probably wrong. After all, he's the doctor, you'd think he would have thought to test you." He sounded doubtful.

I nodded. "How would I know?"

"A plasma test would show," he said. "You'd have to search for the organism—a slow-growing bacteria that eats the lymphatic walls."

"Eats the—what?" I gasped.

"I don't remember exactly," he said. "Again, I'm not an expert."

I was still staring at him when the light from the galley flashed on behind me. Almira's clear, comfortable voice rang out. "Andi! How are you this morning, honey?"

I didn't answer for a moment, then I stammered out, "I'm fine."

"I was just about to start breakfast. Do you need to eat something now, or can you wait?"

I turned and tried to smile at her. "I'll wait," I said.

She glanced inquiringly at Commander Howitz as she pulled an apron off a metal peg just inside the door.

Settling himself more comfortably on his bar stool, he dug an electronic book out of his pocket and set it on the counter. "I'll wait. Are you going to wait, Miss Andi?"

I moved around to the front of the bar and seated myself on a bar stool. "Yes. Thank you for your concern."

He smiled. "I hope I'm wrong, I truly do." He turned on his book and began to read, taking no more notice of me.

I felt dazed as I watched Almira bustle around getting our breakfasts together. This was silly. Of course, if I did have this—this Langham's Disease, the Doctor would have found out long ago. Commander Howitz wasn't even a doctor; what did he know?

I looked at my wrist again. It wasn't swollen. Was it? I couldn't deny the knee pains, however. But could a lymphatic deficiency cause something *that* painful?

I shuddered. Surely not.

I started to reach for a napkin and stopped midway, remembering something.

"Meet me there at nine... I want to test you for something."

Could it be the Langham's Disease that he wanted to test me for? Could he have wondered about my knee pains being related to that?

If he knew I had some disease, why would he hide it from me? That was ridiculous. Besides, Commander Howitz said that I would have died shortly after birth—

"What does it matter what he says?" I mumbled.

"Pardon me?" asked the commander, looking up from his book.

I felt my cheeks flush as I shook my head. "Nothing."

I glanced at a chronometer above the galley door. It wasn't even seven yet, and I felt strangely uncomfortable about going to sickbay before the appointed time. I wasn't positive if he'd want me there, silly as I knew the feeling was.

As Almira served us both, the mess hall began to fill up with hungry crewmembers. The Doctor didn't come down, I noticed as I slowly ate, trying to fill up the time.

When I was done with breakfast I lingered for awhile, then I helped clear the tables. Time dragged on, and when I'd finished helping Almira clean up, it was still fifteen minutes before nine.

She noticed my behavior. "Is everything okay, honey? You seem a bit distracted."

"I'm all right," I said, trying to smile. She must have seen it wasn't true, because she stopped what she was doing to give me a hug. I returned it, but it didn't make me feel any better.

I loitered down the corridors for awhile, waiting for nine to come. I had thought of going to ask if I could help on the bridge, but since I only had about ten minutes before my appointment, I didn't think that was wise.

My appointment. I squirmed a little, then scolded myself again. *Andi Lloyd, I'm ashamed of you! Be sensible and wait to see what the Doctor wants. Stop imagining things.* Like most of my self-scoldings, it didn't help much.

A couple minutes before nine, I finally hurried to sickbay, hoping that he wouldn't mind if I was a couple minutes early. Why should he?

I found him putting a laser away in the main medical cabinet, and he closed the doors as I stepped into the room. I took in the medical atmosphere gladly, letting the familiarity of it relax me a bit.

He looked at me as I approached him, and I noted with concern the weariness of his expression. His face was a little pale, and his eyes lacked their usual sparkle of wit.

"Are you feeling okay?" I asked, frowning.

He didn't try to lie. "I'm sorry Andi... thank you for coming, but I'm just so tired. I don't know what it is."

"Did you sleep well last night?" I suggested.

Shaking his head, he tried to smile. "I guess I've been a little worried."

"If you want to go rest, I could look after things here," I offered.

Before answering, he looked around the room for a moment. "What we need around here is a nurse."

I never liked him to suggest nurses. It was so nice with just him and me. "I can take care of it, Dad."

He turned back and smiled tiredly. "Thank you."

For half a second I forgot why I'd come. Then I saw him start to walk away, and I called, "Wait, Doctor?"

He faced me. "Yes?"

"You wanted to test me for something?"

Sighing, he looked tiredly at me. "Oh yes. Do you mind if we do it later?"

I wanted to ask him for more information, but he looked so weary that I bit my tongue and shook my head. "That's okay."

He smiled gently, which made me more worried than ever. I'd never known him to be so tired. "Thank you, dear."

Nor did he ever call me "dear." I could only nod and watch him leave the room.

A small shudder ran through me, and I couldn't stop it. There were too many strange things happening. Instead of getting better after Crash left, as I'd hoped, they'd only gotten worse, even in the brief few hours he'd been gone.

My eyes drifted to a hypo sitting on a desk a few yards away, and I walked forward and picked it up, an idea firming to a determination in my mind. Commander Howitz had said that I could find out if I had Langham's Disease with a plasma test. I might as well set my mind at rest.

I went to sterilize the hypo.

CHAPTER VIII

"Commander?"

He sat at lunch in the mess hall, eating a sandwich, and looked up when I addressed him. "Hello, Andi! Can I help you?"

I didn't like that he called me "Andi." After all, I'd just met him the day before. But shaking off my feelings, I resolutely held a closed tube out to him. "I need a favor."

"Yes?"

Did he remember our conversation from hours before, I wondered? I'd had to wait until lunch to speak with him, since I couldn't visit engineering. He was practically a stranger, but I didn't know who else to ask. And I needed to know the answer to this.

"I took a blood sample earlier. Could you... could you tell me what to test for? For that disease you told me about?"

He nodded earnestly. "I'd be glad to... though it would be easier for me to test it myself, if you don't mind." Again, his small, dark eyes seemed to search me intensely for a moment.

"I don't mind... I'd be grateful." I handed him the tube. "I didn't think you'd know how."

"I can do more than engineering," he chuckled. "I'm no doctor, but I can manage a few simple things like that. I don't know if I'll have time today—Captain Trent wants the attitude control back online quickly."

"That's perfectly all right," I assured. "Just... whenever you have time."

Nodding, I took a couple steps backwards, and then turned.

His voice stopped me. "Andi?" he said.

I closed my eyes and just said it. "Miss Lloyd, please."

"Miss Lloyd?" he persisted.

"Yes sir?"

"I don't think you should say anything to your father about this."

I bit my lip and turned to face him.

"I don't keep secrets from my father, Commander."

Nodding, he spoke quickly. "I respect that. But I'm worried that he might—" he hesitated here, and I cut him off.

"My father wouldn't hurt me."

"Of course not." Again, that doubtful tone. "But Andi..."

"Miss Lloyd."

"Miss Lloyd, what if you do have it? How could he not have known?"

I couldn't figure out how to answer that, so I pretended he hadn't said it. "Thank you for your help."

This time I walked away, and barely heard him call after me, "You're welcome."

As I walked, I looked around again for the Doctor. Surely he was up now.

A moment's searching among the full tables proved futile, but close observation showed me that neither the Captain nor Guilders were there either. That gave me a pretty good clue as to where they might be.

Not feeling hungry, I trotted out of the room, trying to shake off the tension that I'd felt building up during the conversation with Commander Howitz. Not tension between him and myself—tension within me.

I rode the elevator down to C-Deck, and trotted down the hall to the Captain's quarters at the end of the hall. The door didn't slide open automatically when I approached it, so I pressed the small white button on the wall just to the right. A muffled chime sounded from within, and the Captain called, "Come in, it's unlocked."

I pushed another button to open the door, and it slid upwards, revealing the bright, open room.

A hearty laugh rang out as I stepped in, and I saw the three men I was looking for seated around a small table, each with a drink. A checkers game lay between the Captain and Guilders, half played, but neither of them seemed to have much interest in it. The Doctor sat back in his chair, fingering his glass, and I thought he still looked exhausted. When he saw me, he smiled.

"How are you feeling?" I asked, walking forward.

He shook his head, and the Captain said, "I'm trying to convince him to go lay down. I think he's coming down with something."

As I crossed the room, I glanced around. On the walls hung shelves which displayed mementos of the Captain's past journeys, and a shelf of electronic books, including everything from engineering manuals, to history, to Tennyson and Shakespeare.

The room was well lit, and had a large window on one wall, which at the moment showed the stars flying past. A plain but comfortable bed stood against one wall, and on the other side of the room were two upholstered chairs and a small leather sofa, clustered around a silver heater.

Positioned near the window was the small table, where the Captain and one or both of his close friends often shared a drink. I approached the Doctor and stood behind him, laying a hand on his shoulder.

"Are you all right?"

He shrugged, and I let my hand fall away. "I'm just so tired. Maybe I'm getting too old for this job."

"Oh, nonsense, Gerry." The Captain finished the dregs of his drink and pushed his cup away. "You do a fine job. You're just a little run down. Maybe I'll hire a nurse sometime, let you take a vacation. It's been too long since your last shore leave."

I hated when the talk of nurses came up, and I cut him off as soon as I could without being disrespectful. "Did you get any rest earlier?"

The Doctor shook his head. "I tried, but couldn't sleep."

"Go rest, Gerard," Guilders suggested, pushing his drink aside and moving a checker.

The Doctor shook his head. "I'll go in a minute. What did you need, Andi?"

"Nothing, I just..."

"Would you do me a favor, then?" the Captain asked.

"Yes sir." I straightened up, prepared to take orders.

"It's just that Crewman Baker always forgets to dust my books. I would do it myself, but Guilders wants me to play..."

By Guilders' quiet scoff, I gathered that it was more the other way around, but I smiled. "Of course."

"Cloths are in the cabinet. Thanks, Andi!" The Captain moved his piece.

The Doctor grunted. "Trent, you're a big boy. Can't you keep your room clean yet?"

"Never learned," the Captain said, studying the board.

I reached into a cabinet next to the bookshelf and pulled out a soft dusting cloth. Then I turned to the books. There weren't many of them, but he had more than most people on the ship. Most officers could fit all their titles on one electronic reader, and didn't mind having all of them mixed up together. Not so Captain Trent. He liked to have smaller readers and more of them, and he had them all organized by author. Byron, Dickens, Milton, Plato—he had every classic anyone could name.

As I pulled the books off the shelf one by one, I thought about my own readers. I was not quite as organized, and I owned six readers, five of them full and the sixth still with some room left. I didn't think most of the crew owned any conventional books, other than the Doctor, who distrusted electronic readers and preferred to turn real, paper pages.

I myself had only one conventional book, and I smiled as I imagined the soft brown leather cover underneath my fingers. It was fitting that my most important book should be my only "real" book, I thought.

The conversation over the checkers game went on, the Doctor leaning back and criticizing each move.

"Don't take so long to think, Guilders," the Captain complained as the older man sat observing the board. "I need to get back to the bridge in—" he consulted his wristcom "—ten minutes."

Guilders reached forward and picked up a black checker. "If you took a little longer to think, you might win sometimes." He jumped his piece over two of the Captain's.

The Captain groaned. "I do win sometimes," he protested, handing his pieces over.

"I would think you would have noticed that, Trent," the Doctor scolded.

I smiled as I dusted the books.

"By the way, Gerry," the Captain spoke up after a moment of silence, "what have you found out about Andi's problem—her knee, I mean. What happened on the bridge?"

I didn't turn to look, but a slight shiver tickled down my back in the momentary silence that followed.

"Nothing," the Doctor said. "I mean—something happened, but I don't know what."

His voice dismissed further questioning, and I bit my lip as I dusted a crimson copy of Shakespeare's plays. There was no further conversation for several minutes, and a bold question entered my mind. I had to work up the courage to ask it, so it wasn't until a few books later that I spoke.

"Have any of you ever heard of Langham's Disease?"

For a moment, no one answered. I didn't turn around, but tried to hide my red face among the books.

"No," said the Captain. I hadn't expected him to be the first to speak. "Why do you ask?"

Before I could answer, the Doctor's voice, weary, spoke. "I know something about it."

That was all. The chill of nervousness chased down my spine again. Somehow I didn't want to face him, but I wondered what his expression was. I waited for him to say something else, but he didn't.

I wasn't planning on pursuing the topic further, but Guilders started his own answer to my question.

"My niece and grand-niece were both diagnosed with it, shortly after my grand-niece was born."

This interested me. "What happened?" I asked, still dusting.

"They both died."

CHAPTER IX

His voice was as flat as ever, but it didn't stop my heart from going out to him. I turned around at last and looked at him. "I'm sorry, Guilders."

He nodded and moved a checker. I stole a glance at the Doctor's face, but he wasn't looking at me. He just looked tired.

"What is it?" the Captain asked, taking his turn.

Since Guilders and the Doctor didn't answer, I volunteered the information. "It's a lymphatic disorder. Some congenital organism that eats the lymphatic vessels. I just heard of it today—I don't know that much."

"That doesn't sound enjoyable."

Guilders spoke quietly. "My niece said it wasn't."

I took a step nearer the little group. "You saw her after she was diagnosed?"

"Yes. "

"And there's no cure?"

He shrugged his broad shoulders and jumped another of the Captain's pieces. "I don't know. I heard rumors of a cure being developed about that time, but nothing definite."

The Doctor abruptly stood up. "I'm sorry—I can't focus. I'm so tired. I'm going to have to go try to get some rest."

I nodded, and the Captain said, "Yes, please do, Gerry."

He turned his tired gray eyes on me, and I reproached myself severely for my absurdity, and stepped to his side.

"You can take care of things, Andi?"

"Yes sir."

"I might not come down to dinner. I'm just—so tired."

I nodded once more, then impulsively kissed him on the cheek. "I hope you feel better soon, Dad."

"Thank you." He brushed my arm with his hand, then turned and left the room.

I watched him leave and felt that pang in my heart again.

The Captain shook his head. "Poor Gerry. He is looking old."

Feeling fierce, I wheeled around. "He's not old!"

Shrugging, he stood up. "I suppose I shouldn't talk, when he only has six years on me. I'm heading up, Guilders. Good game."

"I'll come," was all Guilders said.

"Thanks for the dusting, Andi," the Captain smiled.

I tried to return the smile, but didn't think I'd quite succeeded. "Any time."

Guilders walked out, and the Captain gestured me towards the door with a flourish. I smiled half-heartedly and hurried out, then he followed, closed the door, and started towards the elevator.

I wished I hadn't asked that silly question. If the Doctor had heard about it—then how didn't he know I had it?

Stopping in my walk down the hall, I reined my thoughts in firmly. I didn't even know if I had it yet.

As I thought about my earlier meeting with Commander Howitz, I remembered the reason I couldn't seek him in engineering. My knee implant. Surely that had something to do with the pain! It was too much of a coincidence. But why should it just suddenly start hurting, when no impact had ever made it hurt before? And if I did have Langham's Disease, was it just a coincidence that the "sudden, intense joint pain" had occurred in the one joint in my body that was not fully bone?

That kneecap now—that was something of a mystery. It wasn't even the whole kneecap, just a tiny bit of metal implanted in the middle of an otherwise bone patella. I remembered when the Doctor had first told me that I had it.

"Why did I need that?" I'd asked, puzzled.

He'd shaken his head. "I don't know. You had it when I found you."

It had never hurt me before. Why should it start now?

If it was the Langham's Disease that caused it to start hurting—

I couldn't have had the disease since birth, or I would have died.

So it wasn't possible. I dismissed the idea and hurried to sickbay, hoping that there would be work there to calm my overactive imagination.

* * *

I was just drifting off to sleep that night when a beep jolted me awake. I looked around groggily, trying to find out where it was coming from. Whatever it was, it beeped again, and I tried to place the familiar sound.

My wristcom. That was it. Startled, I picked it up and fumbled to get my finger on the button. "Yes?"

No answer. Neither voice nor static came, and as I brought the indicator into focus, I saw that the call had been terminated.

"Must have the wrong number," I mumbled, setting the band down on my nightstand and snuggling under the covers again.

My mind had just begun to wander into dreams when the beep came again, and this time I sat up. I picked up the com and answered. "Hello?"

This time, there was static, and I looked to see who was calling. It was the Doctor's com number.

"Hello?" I said again.

"Andi..." came his voice, weak and forced. Then I heard a grunt that was almost a groan, then the call was terminated again.

Thoroughly aroused, I stood up and reached for the

dressing gown I'd thrown over a chair the night before. Something was wrong with him—I had no idea what, but I knew he needed my help.

Trying to get my bearings, I stumbled towards the door, not taking the time to order lights on. When I reached it, I unlocked it and slipped out into the dim halls, blinking in the faint light.

The Doctor's room was right next to mine, and I pushed the button to open his door. It opened readily, he rarely locked his cabin, even at night. I slipped in and let the door slide shut behind me.

A tiny beam of light from one corner of the room showed me the Doctor's form, tossing and turning on his bed.

Tip-toeing, I made my way to the bed and sat down on the side of it. His face was twisted as if in pain, and I laid my hand gently on his chest. "Doctor?"

He stopped tossing, and his heavy breathing slowed, but his eyes remained closed, and his face didn't change.

In a whisper which was only slightly louder, I said, "Dad?"

The eyes opened and he stared up at me, an empty, dazed stare.

"Dad," I reassured quietly, "It's me. Andi. Don't you know me?"

His eyes remained void, and a voice that was not his own sounded from his throat. "Why do you call me dad?"

My heartbeat accelerated.

An intelligent look spread over his face, and his eyes grew confused. "Andi? What are you doing here?" His voice was back to normal now.

"You called me."

"I called you?" His brow wrinkled in confusion.

I bit my lip. "Yes. Are you all right?"

"Of course." He seemed gruffer than usual. "Just can't sleep, that's all."

"Bad dreams?"

The question seemed to confuse him. He looked up at me

as if he were searching for something, then rested his hand on mine. "Yes."

Somehow, I felt like he meant "no." But I also felt that questioning him further would only make him uncomfortable. "I just wanted to make sure you were all right."

But as I rose to leave, his hand closed around mine spasmodically. "No. No, don't go."

I complied, and sat in silence for a moment. After continuing to search my face for whatever it was he sought, he said, almost pleadingly, "My mother..." He paused, and when he began to speak again, the other voice was back. "...she used to sing me a song when I couldn't sleep. Will you sing it for me?"

His voice sounded so distant—almost lost.

I forced myself to speak calmly and lightly. "Do you know the name of the song?"

After searching my face again, he said, "No. Will you sing it for me?"

My hand trembled, but I again calmed myself. "I do not know the song your mother sang, but I will sing for you."

His hold on my hand relaxed, and I began to softly sing him a lullaby. But before the first verse was over, I felt his body relax, his eyes closed, and his breathing became regular again. After I had finished the song, I whispered, "Goodnight, Dad," and, leaning forward, planted a kiss on his cheek before rising to leave.

Extremely shaken, I made my way back to my room, shut and locked the door, and dropped onto my bed, breathing deeply and feeling my heart race.

I didn't think I would be able to sleep at all after that. What did it mean? What was the unrest in his face? I'd never seen anything like it before. It made me so uneasy, that I had more than half a mind to go get the Captain. But it was so late, and I shrank from waking him.

Tomorrow, I would find out what was going on, somehow.

CHAPTER X

I didn't know I had drifted off to sleep until my alarm awakened me. That meant it was seven thirty. Apparently I had been able to sleep after all.

Laying there in the dimness, I recalled the night before in my mind. I wanted to think it had only been a dream, but I knew I couldn't do that. I could almost feel the moist pressure of the Doctor's hand on mine as he begged me to sing for him, and hear the strange note of distance and confusion in his voice.

No longer would I be able to convince myself that things would get themselves back to normal. I would have to do something—what, I wasn't sure yet. First I needed to figure out what was wrong with the Doctor.

As I jumped up and dressed, I tried to figure out just what to say to him. Should I just ask him right out what had happened last night? Or see if he brought it up first? I didn't quite like to just walk up and say, "Hey Dad, what was wrong with you last night?" What if it had only been a bad dream, like he said? On the whole, I thought it would be better just to ask him in a less direct way—perhaps just see if he was still acting strangely, or if he referred to it himself.

Strapping on my wristcom, I hurried out the door and rode the elevator up to B-Deck.

As I trotted to sickbay, I took a couple of deep breaths to calm myself down. Then, straightening my jacket, I peeked in.

He was there, giving a crewman his regular checkup. Evidently he hadn't seen me come in, and I stood there observing him for a moment. It seemed to me that his hair was a little bit grayer than a few days ago, and his always thin form seemed even thinner. The lines on his forehead had multiplied, and his frown was more frequent than ever.

As I stood observing him, the patient got up, thanked him, and walked towards the door. I stepped aside, and the man passed me with a nod. The Doctor began changing the sheets.

Stepping into the room with purpose, I forced myself to call brightly, "Good morning, Dad."

He looked up quickly, and then said, "Good morning."

Hesitantly, I stepped a little closer. "Are you feeling better this morning?"

"Better?"

He looked confused, standing there with one corner of the clean sheet in his hands, staring.

"You know... you were tired yesterday."

"Oh yes." He went back to putting the new sheets on. "I think Trent was right. I just need a break. I might ask him to go ahead and hire a nurse..."

"No!" I said.

He looked at me, frowning.

I blushed and looked down. "I mean... we don't need a nurse. We can take care of things by ourselves. Just you and me."

Sneaking a look at his face, I found his eyes fixed steadily on me.

"Let me help you with that," I mumbled, and moved forward to tuck the corners of the sheet under the cot mattress.

He stepped back and let me work.

"Did you sleep well last night?" I asked, remembering the strange incident.

It was a moment before he answered, just long enough for anxiety to begin to rise in my chest.

"Like a log," he said at last.

I shivered. I should ask him about it. Now. But—did he not remember? Or did he just not want to talk about it? Other than a slightly absent manner, he appeared to be acting normal.

My mouth felt dry, and I tried to decide what to say next. Never had I felt so awkward around him.

"What were you asking about yesterday?"

I knew what he meant, but still I asked, "What do you mean?"

"In Trent's quarters. You asked me something. What was it?"

He sounded lost again. Confused—searching.

"Langham's Disease," I said, trying to sound cheerful and careless, but with a vague feeling that I was failing.

"Yes—that was it." He didn't say anything else, didn't ask why I'd wanted to know, nothing. He said nothing at all.

"Should we go to breakfast?" I asked, struggling to speak lightly.

"I need to wash my hands," he said, standing up. "You go ahead without me."

Part of me protested against leaving him, but I agreed and left the room, heart sinking quickly. Something was wrong.

I sat by myself at a little round table in the mess hall, idly picking at my food. It occurred to me as I moved the eggs back and forth with my fork that I had not told the Doctor about the Langham's Disease test I'd asked Commander Howitz to help me with. I hadn't intended to keep it a secret from him; I'd meant it when I told the Commander that I wouldn't. Yet somehow, I couldn't bring myself to say anything about it. Why, I did not know exactly. It just seemed that if I said anything about it—well, he'd know that I'd doubted him. And then if he had done nothing wrong, it would hurt him. If he had—

Well, that's what Commander Howitz was afraid of.

Maybe he was right. What harm could it do to not tell him, or at least not yet?

My conscience pricked me, hard. Was that fair to him? When had he ever done anything to deserve this distrust? He was my father, after all.

He's not your real father.

I felt like slapping myself. Yes he was! It didn't matter if he wasn't my biological father. He was the one who had trained me, provided for me, cared for me for my whole life.

But it was all so hard to explain.

"Miss Lloyd?"

Startled, I looked up and saw young August Howitz standing in front of my table, a piece of paper in his hands.

"Yes?"

He held the paper out to me. "My father asked me to give you this. He had to do some work on one of the airlocks, but wanted to get it to you as soon as possible."

To my frustration, I found myself reddening with guilt as I took the paper. I should show this to the Doctor. It was probably the notes on the blood test.

"Thank you." I took the paper and folded it, then slipped it into my jacket pocket. Nervously, I pushed a slip of hair behind my ear and turned back to my food.

"Are you feeling better?" he asked.

I nodded. "Yes, thank you." I felt my skin turning even hotter as I realized how my behavior must look to the young man. I looked up and tried to smile. "Forgive me if I'm being rude. I'm just—tired."

Nodding, he said, "I understand. I heard that your father has not been feeling well—it must have been quite a strain on you."

"I can handle it," I assured. "He'll be fine."

"I'm sure he will."

I nodded, and went on pretending to eat.

"Can I do anything for you, Miss Lloyd?"

The tone was kind and respectful, and it put me more at ease and softened my heart. I smiled more gratefully this time. "No, but thank you for your concern."

He smiled back, then turned and left.

There were few people left in the room, I observed.

Perhaps a half dozen officers, one of whom was the Captain, who sat near the doorway finishing the last few bites of his breakfast.

My stomach rumbled, and I looked down at my food and wrinkled my nose. I didn't want to eat, but I needed to. Laying my fork down, I picked up a piece of bacon and prepared to bite it.

"Gerry!"

The Captain's voice was tinged with concern, and I jerked my head in his direction.

In the doorway, the Doctor stood. I couldn't see him well that far away, with the light behind him, but he seemed to stagger slightly as he walked, and his shoulders drooped. Dropping the bacon, I jumped up and raced towards him.

The Captain was at his side in a moment. "Gerry, you look awful. You're sweating..."

From this distance I could see moisture dotting his face, but he shook his head. "No, I was just washing my face. I'm all right, Trent."

He tried to push the Captain away and start towards a chair, but the Captain held firmly to his arm. "Gerry, you're not well. You need rest."

The Doctor grunted. "I'm the doctor, not you."

"As your commanding officer, I order you..." He stopped when he saw me hurrying up. "Andi, you can convince him."

I stared. The Captain was right, he *did* look awful. He was pale, except for the two dark half-circles under his eyes, and his eyes had a glazed-over look. His face was moist, as were his hands, and when he looked at me, he looked as though he was trying to find his way.

"Where's Crash?" he asked. "He was here just now, wasn't he?"

I froze, staring into his eyes. He still looked lost, and I spoke slowly. "Crash left, Doctor. He left yesterday morning."

"Left? But he was just here..."

What was wrong with him? He was acting the same way he had the night before, only worse. It was disturbing, and a wave of panic swept over me. Was he going crazy? Or was he developing some kind of psychosis? I couldn't bear the thought of anything happening to my beloved Doctor. I just couldn't even stand to let the thought cross my mind.

I touched his hand. "Dad, what's wrong?"

His eyes suddenly cleared, and some color washed into his face. "Wrong? I'm only tired, Andi. Trent, what are you holding onto me for?"

The Captain and I exchanged a worried look, and he opened his mouth to speak, but a voice from his wristcom intercepted him.

"Airlock prepared for mooring, sir." I recognized the voice of Commander Howitz.

The Captain let go of his friend to answer the call. "I'll be right there, Mr. Howitz." He switched frequencies and said, "Mr. Yanendale, give permission to moor."

"Aye sir."

Turning the com off, the Captain spoke clearly and firmly. "Gerry, if you won't listen to reason, I'm going to have to confine you to quarters."

"Don't be ridiculous, Trent. I'm only tired..."

"Dad," I begged.

He looked at me, and I saw confusion still hiding behind his eyes. But he didn't complain any more.

The Captain laid a hand on his arm. "Come on, Gerry."

I waited, my hand on his, anxious to hear his response. He looked from one of us to the other, paused, then relaxed. "All right. I am tired."

Letting go of him, the Captain turned to me. "See that he gets to his quarters all right, Andi."

"Yes sir."

"I don't see what the fuss is about..." the Doctor grumbled.

"Please, Dad." I looked up into his eyes for a moment. He sighed, and let me lead him out of the mess hall.

"I'm hungry," he began when we were a few feet down the corridor.

"I'll get you something, Doctor."

Nodding, he kept silent for the rest of the walk to his cabin. He lay down without complaint, and nodded again when I said, "I'll be right back with your breakfast."

I hurried out of the room, heart pounding. My hands shook, and I tried to take calm, slow breaths. "Just tired" wasn't good enough any more. Something was the matter.

CHAPTER XI

Almira was kind enough to fix a tray of eggs and bacon for the Doctor, even though she had finished cooking and begun cleaning up. I took the meal down to him.

"Thank you," was all he said, and he didn't look like he wanted to talk. A pang pierced my heart as I watched him slowly begin eating the eggs. What had happened to the energetic, witty Doctor of a few days ago?

"Can I get you anything?" I asked softly.

Shaking his head, he focused his eyes on mine for a moment. "Just look after sickbay for me."

I nodded, two quick nods. "I will."

As he turned back to his food, something seemed to stop him. He looked back at me, searchingly, but instead of looking at my face, he looked at my jacket pocket. "What's that?"

"What?" I asked, forgetting. Then I reddened as I remembered the paper from Commander Howitz. A corner of it stuck out of my jacket. I should tell the Doctor about it, show him, let him figure out the mystery with me.

"It's nothing," I mumbled, stuffing it back into my pocket.

Without even questioning, he went back to his eggs. I swallowed, opened my mouth, then turned and fled, not waiting to make sure the door slid closed behind me.

I slipped into my room, not allowing myself time to stop and think, and I pulled the paper out of my pocket. Then I stood holding it and observing my accelerated heartbeat for a moment. Closing my eyes tightly, I opened the paper, then looked at it.

It was the blood test results, just as I'd thought. I skimmed over the automatic results, things I already knew. Blood type, red blood cell count, etc. It was the special searches that I was interested in.

I had tried doing some research on Langham's disease on the Doctor's electronic magazines, but had been unable to find anything beyond vague references. Commander Howitz hadn't been lying when he said that it was obscure. I didn't know what the organism in Langham's Disease was called, but out of the corner of my eye I saw some black, cramped handwriting at the bottom of the page, and assumed he'd explained. Eagerly, I read over the plasma report and noted the small cell count of "angiophages."

Gripping the paper, I put the word together in my mind. Angio—vessel. Phage—eating. Eating vessels. That wasn't a hard one to figure out.

My gaze drifted to the bottom of the page, and I strove to make out the Commander's small, inky handwriting.

"Presence of angiophages detected, though in small amounts. Not sure what to make of this. Will find you at lunch. Erasmus Howitz."

That wasn't much of an explanation, but he did say he would speak to me at lunch. Gritting my teeth, I ripped the paper into two pieces, wadded them both up viciously, then hurled them into the recyclator chute next to the lavatory. Then I sighed.

My wristcom beeped, and Captain Trent's voice sounded from it. "Andi? Did you get him settled?"

"Yes sir. He's resting now. I was just on my way up to sickbay."

"Could you do me a favor first?"

"Yes sir."

"We have some guests in airlock one, but we're in the middle of a warp test right now and I can't leave the bridge. Would you welcome them aboard please?"

"Certainly."

"Mr. Yanendale is coming down, too. The visitors are looking for someone—they think he might be here. No, Guilders, wait a second! Sorry, Andi... I don't want them wandering around my ship until I talk to them, so you and Yanendale take them to the briefing room on C-Deck, all right?"

"Yes sir, I'll do that," I assured, already starting out the door.

"Thank you. Tell them I'll meet them there in twenty minutes. Hold on, keep course..."

The call was cut off, and I raced down the hall and up the elevator towards airlock one, heart beating nervously. Looking for someone? I shuddered as I remembered the warning Doctor Holmes had sent via Crash.

"What would they want with an old country doctor?"

They couldn't be here for him. And if they were, then they were mistaken in thinking—

Thinking what? What did they think?

I pushed these thoughts away and hastened to obey the Captain's request.

Lieutenant Commander Yanendale was already at the airlock when I reached it, and he nodded briskly as I approached. Moving his fingers over the keypad to the left of the airlock entrance, he unsealed it and then stepped back, hands behind his back, legs apart.

I stood up straight and put my hands by my side, trying to look proper and military as the large door slid open noisily to reveal two men.

One of them was tall, with broad shoulders and a thick, set jaw. The other, a little behind him, was significantly shorter, hardly more than my height. He had bright eyes that seemed to be too high on his forehead, a small nose that was turned up slightly, and he stepped out of the airlock with a strange gait that made it look as though one leg was shorter than the other. They were both dressed in some kind of blue uniform, with a silver insignia that I didn't recognize, but Yanendale appeared to.

"Lieutenant Commander Yanendale, comm marshal of the

starship *Surveyor.*"

He glanced at me, and I bowed slightly. "And I'm Andi Lloyd, second medical officer. Welcome aboard, gentlemen."

The tall man barely nodded, and flashed a badge from inside his jacket. "Oliver Peat, special agent of the ILA. This is my partner, Mr. Sigmet."

"Welcome," Yanendale echoed. "Captain Trent will see you in the briefing room in a moment."

"Won't you come this way?" I said, hoping I sounded formal and courteous enough. I wasn't used to welcoming official visitors, and I certainly wasn't used to speaking with agents of the International Legal Association. These must not be the men Crash had warned about.

After I gestured in the general direction of the briefing room, Yanendale began to walk there, and I smiled at the two men before following. Peat didn't change his expression in the least, but Sigmet, as he began limping along in his strange way, did. At least, his mouth did, curving up in a broad smile. His eyes didn't change at all.

They both unnerved me. I turned away from them, and found myself reassured by the familiarity even of the back of Yanendale's green jacket.

We led them a little way down the hall and into the white briefing room. Yanendale stood aside to let them in the door, then gestured to the seats at the long, white table.

Without waiting for further invitation, they both selected seats about halfway down the room and sat. They didn't speak to us, but just sat patiently staring ahead. I found myself feeling more awkward, and a sidelong glance at Yanendale showed me that he wasn't feeling entirely comfortable himself. He cleared his throat. "The Captain should be here soon."

Peat nodded, and Sigmet smiled with his mouth only again, but neither of them said anything.

After another silent moment had passed, I spoke up, my voice sounding small and immature. "Can I get you gentlemen anything?"

"An interview with Captain Trent," said Peat calmly.

I blushed. "I mean... could I get you a drink or something?"

"No thank you."

Even if I'd wanted to speak again, I couldn't think of anything else to say. So we stayed as we were, the two agents sitting silently, Yanendale and I standing on either side of the open door, waiting.

It seemed like hours before the Captain finally walked through the door, standing straight and tall, his tanned face serious and captain-like, with his green cap perched staunchly on top of his head. The two guests stood up when he entered.

"I'm Captain Harrison Trent," he said, advancing to shake hands with the two men.

"Oliver Peat, special agent of the ILA," said Peat, with exactly the same intonations he'd used when introducing himself to us. "This is my assistant Mr. Sigmet."

The Captain furrowed his brows. "What is the trouble?"

Mr. Sigmet spoke up quickly, as if to reassure him. "It has nothing to do with you or your ship, Captain."

Rather than responding, the Captain turned around. "Yanendale, you may return to your station."

The comm marshal nodded and left. I was about to turn and leave, but the Captain's voice stopped me. "Wait, Andi, my com is out of batteries. Would you go replace them and ask Guilders to report here as soon as he can? And bring it back when you're done." As he spoke, he unstrapped his wristcom and held it out to me.

"Yes sir." Taking it, I hurried on my way to the hold, where extra supplies of all kinds were kept. On the way, I gave Guilders the Captain's message via my wristcom, and when I reached the hold I hurriedly replaced the batteries in the com. Then I rushed back up the elevator to C-Deck and to the briefing room.

Guilders wasn't there yet, but the Captain was deep in conversation with the two agents when I entered.

"I don't care if you have a warrant, he's under my authority and my protection, and I'll have to verify your story before I can allow you to make an arrest."

"But you have no way of verifying it," Sigmet protested. "You're not in range of the comm towers."

"We will be, in four more sectors, and you will just have to wait until then."

Peat stood and drew himself up to his full height, eyes indignant. "But Trent, Erasmus Howitz is a dangerous criminal!"

CHAPTER XII

I stood, frozen, in the doorway, the Captain's wristcom laying in my hand. The Captain furrowed his brows and stood up, almost matching Peat's height.

"I'm sorry, but I will have to verify your story. Commander Howitz is not going anywhere, you can stay here until we reach sector fifty-one-forty."

"Excuse me, Miss Andi."

It was Guilders' voice, from behind me, and I felt his hand laid politely on my shoulder. I realized then that I was in his way, and I scooted aside, feeling vaguely confused. Then I remembered why I had come here. "Your com, Captain," I said, stepping forward.

He reached out and took it, and I could see frustration behind his eyes. He liked Commander Howitz, and the cold insistence of these men clashed with his normal routine. "Thank you. You may go attend sickbay now."

I nodded, wishing that I could in good conscience take that as a suggestion rather than a command to leave the room. But when the Captain gave suggestions, they were to be obeyed, as I had learned long ago, and so I turned and left, feeling my own frustration as the door slid closed behind me.

I trudged to sickbay, wondering just what Peat had meant by saying "Erasmus Howitz is a dangerous criminal." What had he done? Could these men have any motive for lying? And yet the Captain clearly considered it at least a possibility, if not likely.

My pager beeped as I walked down the hall, jolting me out

of my thoughts. There was no reason for me to worry about it. It didn't concern me at all. All I needed to do right now was take care of sickbay so that the Doctor could get his rest. Later, perhaps at dinner, I would talk to the Captain about what had been happening with the Doctor, the strange way he had been acting. The Captain would know what to do.

Only one of the cots was occupied when I walked in, but it was a serious injury. It was a lieutenant from recycling in the hold, who had a nasty gash in his leg. It had gotten caught in the recyclators, and I tried to keep from grimacing after I cut the bloody pant leg away and saw that the cut ran down to the bone. This would require too much regen for a simple local anesthetic. I'd need a full-scale tranquilizer.

An hour after I'd begun work on the man, I was still working on the muscle. Lost in concentration, I focused on positioning the tissue in place with gloved fingers, then injecting the regen shot and letting it work while I moved onto another section. This type of work was on the edge of my healing abilities, and I was glad there was nothing worse. If it were, I would have had to call the Doctor, or if he was unable to work, we might have to stop and try to get help from another ship's medical personnel or a hospital station.

"Miss Lloyd?"

The voice startled me out of my focus for an instant, but I then took a deep breath and closed the last section of muscle. "I'm sorry, I can't talk right now. You'll have to wait until I'm finished here."

I couldn't spare the brain power to wonder about the speaker, or even try to identify the voice. It was a male, that was as much as I had time to notice before I started work closing the skin. This was easier than the muscle, and would hold better, but it was still a difficult task, and I had to finish before the anesthetic wore off.

When at last the cut was closed, only a long, white line gave evidence of the cut, and I wrapped the leg in gauze to keep the tender muscle and skin from tearing during the rest of the regeneration. Then at last, sucking a deep breath through the mask that covered my mouth and nose, I stood up straight and pulled my gloves off, shut off the monitor, and pulled my mask down. Then I turned in the general direction the voice had spoken from.

On one of the cots at the other side of the room, sat August Howitz, his dark eyes wide.

I smiled as I untied my medical tunic and pulled it off. "What is it?"

"That looks hard," he said.

"It is." I dropped the tunic in the laundry chute, and the gloves and mask in the recyclator. Then I pulled my uniform jacket off a metal peg on the wall. "Is that all you needed?"

"No—my father sent me to see if you were all right. He said he was supposed to meet you at lunch."

At the mention of lunch, my stomach began rumbling. "What time is it?"

"It's past two o' clock." He stood up as I walked towards him. "Can I get you something? You seem busy."

I shook my head. "I'm done now, thanks. He'll have to rest for awhile. Is your dad already at work?"

"Yes." He fell into step beside me as I walked to the mess hall. "He said he'll talk to you later."

Hungry as I was, I was somewhat relieved that I'd missed my "appointment." I had no strong desire to talk to Commander Howitz at the moment, though I was still curious about what he had to say to me. And I couldn't forget Peat's voice yelling, *"Erasmus Howitz is a dangerous criminal!"* I sighed.

"Is everything all right, Miss Lloyd?" August said politely.

"Yes," I lied. "I'm—only tired."

"My father seemed worried about you."

"I know. I appreciate his concern, but I'm fine."

He wasn't finished. "I think it had something to do with the men who came aboard earlier."

I stopped, letting him go on a few steps before I hurried to catch up. This—didn't seem to make sense. I couldn't figure out why, but it just didn't seem to add up somehow. Worried about *me* because of our visitors? But they were here for him. Weren't they?

"What makes you say that?" I asked.

He shrugged. "I don't know, he just asked if I'd seen the visitors, and asked me a lot of questions about them, then asked if they'd seen you, and then he said I should go check on you."

Frowning, I walked into the mess hall. August stopped inside the doorway. "So—you're all right?"

"I'm fine," I promised. "Tell your dad I'm all right, and I'll talk to him later."

With a nod that was almost more like a bow, he walked away towards the elevator, and I made a rush for the snack bar, to get something to eat before it closed.

Almira was too busy to talk, so I grabbed a sandwich and some milk and hurried back to sickbay. When I got there, I dismissed the lieutenant to rest in his quarters, then I spread a napkin on the floor, and sat cross-legged to eat.

As I bit into the sandwich, I listened to the silence. There were no monitors active, no scanners running. More than that, there was no warm, gruff voice to comment on my work, or banter with me, or quiz me on medicine and theology. That was the loneliest part of the silence. I was so rarely lonely since we came to space—

"Miss Lloyd, isn't it?"

I jumped up, almost knocking my milk over, and looked around towards the doorway. There stood Peat and Sigmet, the newcomers.

"That's my name," I said, brushing the crumbs off my jacket. "Can I help you?"

Instead of immediately answering, Peat turned his head towards his shorter companion. Sigmet stood behind him, and in his hands was a small metal object, about the size of a book, whirring. Nodding, he pushed a button on the object and it became silent. "That's her, all right."

This vague statement made me nervous, and I backed up a step or two. "May I help you?" I said more loudly, as if that would make him simply answer my question and leave.

Instead, Peat took a step forward. Sigmet didn't move from the doorway. It was as if he were guarding the room.

"We need to have a word with you, Miss Lloyd."

Hands shaking, I moved a finger to the transmission button on my wristcom, but he stopped me with a deep, strong voice. "Don't worry, we won't hurt you."

I didn't move my finger, but he went on. "There's something you need to know—but you're going to have to promise not to tell anyone what I'm about to tell you."

A shiver ran through me as I shook my head. "I can't promise that."

"Then I'm afraid we can't tell you."

"All right," I said, although part of me cried out at the thought of not knowing.

His face darkened in frustration. "You could be in serious danger, Miss Lloyd."

All I could do was shake my head. There didn't seem to be any answer to that—but I would not make a promise I would not keep, and I would not keep any secret that these two had to offer. I'd kept enough secrets already.

He turned back to look at Sigmet again. The smaller man raised one eyebrow in a way that seemed to speak of urgency. With an impatient sigh, Peat turned back to me again, his broad jaw more set than ever.

"All right. You must know—but please, if you value your life, use discretion before you tell anyone else."

I glanced up in the direction of the security camera in the corner of the room, and he spoke quickly. "We've taken care of that. There will be no record of this conversation."

Taking a deep breath, I tried to listen calmly, though I kept one finger near my wristcom. "Tell me."

"Close the door," Peat ordered, and Sigmet obeyed. Then the larger man gestured to one of the cots, while Sigmet limped over to us with his peculiar, lopsided walk.

Slowly, I lowered myself to the cot, never taking my eyes off the two men. They sat across from me, and if it were not for my anxiety, I might have been tempted to laugh at the sight of the two of them, such different heights and aspects, sitting side by side on the cot. But I neither laughed nor smiled.

Contrary to my expectation, Sigmet began the explanation, his bright, high eyes glinting at me. "Is it true that your right patella is partially composed of some metallic substance?"

I started back. That wasn't what I'd been expecting at all. "Yes," I answered.

"And is it true that this metal was already in place when your current father found you?"

For some reason his use of the word "current" bugged me, but I replied in the affirmative, adding, "Why do you want to know?"

At this point, Peat leaned in a little closer, and spoke in a low tone. "We know something about that metal, Miss Lloyd."

"How could you possibly..."

"Let me finish." He sat back again and spoke seriously, mechanically, his thick jaw working through the words as if they were parts on an assembly line. "Have you heard of radialloy?"

I shook my head.

"I thought not. It was a very secret operation." He turned expectantly to Sigmet, who began speaking.

"Radialloy is very valuable. It was discovered over twenty years ago—a metal with extreme destructive abilities. In the hands of the right people—or the wrong people, as the case may be—its damage could easily rival that of the atomic bomb."

He must have seen my eyes widen, for he nodded seriously. "It's an alloy mined from the planet Qandon, in the Gamma quadrant of sector sixteen-forty-one. Shortly after the mine was discovered, however, the planet's sun went nova, and the planet was destroyed, along with all the radialloy."

Here he paused for too long, and I cleared my throat and asked, "But what does this have to do with..."

Mr. Peat interrupted me. "Miss Lloyd, only one specimen of the alloy had been taken from the planet before it was destroyed. Those familiar with it never knew what had happened to the piece. But we have reason to believe that it was hidden, hidden somewhere no one would suspect, with the intention of being able to retrieve it later."

"Hidden..." I stammered, trying to make sense out of the story.

"We believe that it was hidden in your knee."

For a moment, no one spoke. I kept perfectly still, trying to take in all that they had just said. It didn't make sense—did it? Could it really be true? That someone had hidden a dangerous metal in my knee, and that they would be hunting it down? Wanting it back?

"Why did you say I was in danger?" I asked, noticing a tremble in my voice.

"Because some people would do anything to get their hands on it," Peat said. "Our supervisor wants it destroyed before anyone can get to it. We were sent to get it."

"But—" I stammered, "I thought you said you were here to arrest Commander Howitz."

"That's the other thing," Sigmet began, but at that instant, the door slid open. I jumped, and the two men turned their heads in one motion.

CHAPTER XIII

Commander Howitz stood in the doorway, his large frame seeming to fill it, his thick, dark eyebrows drawn angrily over his small, dark eyes.

"Did you gentlemen require anything?" he asked, and for once I welcomed his gravelly voice.

Peat raised himself to his full height and squared his shoulders, but the Commander was a match for him in both height and weight, and the effect was not as intimidating as before.

There was a second of silence, during which the two men looked each other hard in the eyes and I squirmed under the palpable distrust. Sigmet stood and said, "We were just leaving, thank you."

He led the way out the door. After another second of hard staring, Peat followed, not giving so much as a glance in my direction as he exited.

After they had gone, the Commander breathed a low sigh, and relaxed his shoulders slightly. "Were they bothering you?" he asked.

Neither "no" nor "yes" seemed like an appropriate answer, so I kept silent and merely shrugged.

Seating himself on the cot they'd vacated, he looked me straight in the eyes. Only for a moment, and then I dropped my gaze, unable to meet his.

"What did they say to you?"

I couldn't help telling him. It was all so confusing—I didn't know what to do. I wanted to run right to the Doctor and get him to sort it out for me, but he was acting so strange, I knew he couldn't help.

When I finished the story, the Commander looked hard at me for a moment, then his expression softened slightly. He almost, *almost* looked caring, but there was something—something I couldn't explain—that still made me uncomfortable.

"Should I believe them?" I asked at last.

He shook his head vehemently. "No. They're lying."

This was reassuring. It was what I'd wanted to think. "How do you know?"

In response, he kept on looking at me for a moment. Then, he reached out and touched my hand.

I jerked it back, heart racing, but he acted like I hadn't moved.

"It's a half-truth, Andi..."

"Miss Lloyd."

He ignored this. "There is a substance called radialloy, and it was discovered on Qandon. The sun did go nova, and the source was destroyed. You do have the only remaining specimen in your knee."

I felt like I couldn't breathe. "Then... what..."

"It isn't what they said it was."

"It's... it's not dangerous?"

"No. In fact, it's the exact opposite."

"Wh-what do you mean?"

"You remember when I spoke to you about Langham's Disease?"

"Yes."

"You do have it. But it's not a recent thing. You have had it ever since you were a baby. The radialloy is the cure."

The cure. The cure Guilders had spoken of. But—but—

"How do you know this?"

He reached for me again, but I slid further back. Again, he ignored my question. "Those men—whatever they are calling themselves—they only want it for the money, Andi."

"And—if they get it?"

"If they take it, you will die."

Goosebumps tickled over my skin as I tried not to shiver. "Then..."

"But it doesn't have to be that way. Andi, as long as you have it, you'll never be safe. People will always be trying to take it. But I know another cure. I can help you. Let me remove it, let me protect you, and I'll give you the cure. You'll be safe."

Something in his voice made me want to scream. Every instinct was telling me I should use my wristcom, call the Doctor or the Captain... "Why do you want to help me?"

"Because I love you, Andi."

The world seemed to turn gray. I groped for my wristcom, but he clutched my arm and spoke quickly, his gravelly voice cutting through my confusion.

"No—no, you don't understand. I have the right—I loved your mother... you're so much like her, Andi. So much like her."

No, no, it can't be, God, please... "What do you mean?"

"Andi—my Genevieve. I'm your father."

Blindly, I tried to pull my arm away. My throat went dry as he spoke the words I was already expecting. "That can't be..."

"Yes it can. It's true."

"But the Doctor..."

"I don't know why he took you from me—but I can only assume he wanted the cure. He knew if he could find a way to recreate it, he'd..."

"I don't believe you!" I shouted. I wrenched my arm away and stood up. "How can you even know that? How can you know who my father is?"

"Andi, Andi." He smiled. "You have the radialloy. I detected it. And besides—that blood you gave me. I tested the DNA. I wanted to be sure."

"Does the Doctor know... who you are?"

He frowned instantly. "Please, don't talk about him. Genevieve..."

"And why do you keep calling me Genevieve?" I darted for a medical cabinet without thinking. Flinging it open, I dug for nothing in particular.

"Because that's your name." I heard his footsteps approach behind me. "Genevieve Sandison."

"Sandison?" I turned to face him in my surprise.

"I had to change my name—they were coming after me for the radialloy, the same as they did for you."

"But how did they know about me? How... why..." I broke off, not knowing what to say, and allowed myself to meet his eyes for the first time since his revelation.

He advanced, slowly, and put his hands gently on my shoulders. "I don't know. But we'll figure it out. We'll figure it out together."

Oh Doctor! my heart cried, but he kept on talking.

"I'm sorry I brought this on you—but I did it to save you, Genevieve. You have no idea how hard it was to find the cure..."

"Don't call me Genevieve."

He let go of me and frowned.

"And I want to see the DNA match for myself."

He sighed, and an expression I couldn't understand —something like frustration—took over his face. "I suppose it's only natural that you should doubt. But... I've wanted to find you for so long."

"Show me the DNA records." I didn't doubt—I couldn't. I knew it—knew in my very soul that he was my father. My real father. But I wanted, more than anything, to doubt him. If he was telling the truth—how could I ever trust the Doctor again?

"I have them with me." He brushed my arm again, and I found myself wanting to pull away. "I will keep you safe, Andi. I promise."

I turned away. I didn't want to look at him. As he pulled the paper out of his pocket, I cried out inwardly again. *God, it's not true! It's not!*

He handed me another computer printout, and I grabbed it

and read every line of it. That was my blood record. And the DNA reading matched his.

"Does... August know?" I gasped. I wanted to be alone. I wanted to run to my room, to hide, to pray. To implore God to wake me up.

Was everything I knew a lie after all?

"I didn't say anything to August about it. It broke the boy's heart to lose you in the first place, and I didn't want to get his hopes up until I'd talked to you. You can tell him if you like."

I hated listening to his voice. He'd ruined everything about my life. But—but—he was my father. He was. And he was trying to help me.

A sob broke from my throat.

He touched my shoulder. "I understand if you need some time alone."

"I do."

Standing up, he folded the DNA readouts and put them back in his uniform pocket. "I'm sorry I had to tell you this way, Andi. If only those two hadn't..."

"It's all right. I understand." I didn't care why he'd done things the way he had, I only wanted to be alone.

"I'll see you later," he replied, and then he left.

I sank to the floor, crying quietly. How could the world change in only ten minutes? Nothing would ever be right again. I tried hard to sort out my thoughts and emotions about what had just passed, but failed. I gave up at last and just kept crying, my knees drawn up to my chest.

Of everything I'd learned in the two conversations, what bothered me most was not that I had had a deadly disease since birth, that I now had people after me to take the cure for that disease away, or that the unnerving Commander Howitz, who I barely knew, was my father. What bothered me most was the Doctor.

My father was alive, and fully able to care for me, so who could have left me on the Doctor's doorstep? But then—how had he *really* gotten me? And why?

The only solution I could think of was the one the Commander had suggested. The Doctor wanted to figure out how to recreate the cure for himself.

But if that was the case—had he even tried? If he'd tried, wouldn't I have known about it? Unless he'd only done it when I was very little, and had then given up.

Thinking back over our years together, and the many ways he'd cared for me, could I really believe that he would intentionally hurt me?

I recalled the two faces, side by side in my mind. Commander Howitz, smiling, with his small dark eyes and short dark hair, and the thick eyebrows raised at me. Then the Doctor, thin face, gray eyes looking lovingly into mine, and one corner of his mouth raised in an affectionate smile.

Raising my head, I sniffed. "God," I whispered. It was all I said out loud, all I could bring myself to say, but I figured He'd understand. I needed Him, badly, more than I'd ever needed him before. I hadn't felt the need for His help lately—but I did now, more than I'd ever needed anything in my life.

There were still so many unanswered questions. Why had my knee suddenly begun hurting, when the radialloy had never bothered me before? I'd had a few twinges in that knee about a month ago, but they were so mild I'd thought nothing of it. What had happened to my mother? Should I tell the Captain about Peat and Sigmet? Should I let Commander Howitz take the radialloy? And should I leave here with him?

Misery swept over me. I didn't think I could stand being with him for the rest of my life—leaving everything I'd ever known and loved behind.

I stayed there for a long time, just sitting, thinking, praying. I had only wanted things to go back to the way they had been—the way I loved—but now, that was impossible.

"Doctor Lloyd?"

I jumped up, and out of habit began to look for the Doctor,

before remembering that he wasn't there. I rubbed my rough sleeve across my eyes and tried to speak calmly to the pale officer who stood in the doorway. "The Doctor is resting. Is there something I can help you with?"

He only needed a mild burn looked after, and I was glad to be able to bury myself in helping him, and not just sit there feeling sorry and confused and frightened.

It took longer than it should have, and it must have been over an hour later that I had finally dismissed him and begun changing the sheets. With every motion, my thoughts went to the Doctor. I was used to him being there when I worked—sometimes commenting, sometimes asking my help, sometimes saying nothing, just working, the two of us.

How was he doing now? I was afraid to find out. But I was starting to feel that if I didn't talk to somebody about what was going on, I was going to explode.

Without thinking, I let my feet carry me out of sickbay. It was too painful to stay there, since I couldn't look at anything without thinking of the Doctor and my conflicting feelings and beliefs about him. I went on, down the hall, into the elevator, and up the elevator to A-Deck, and from there to the bridge.

I slipped in, wishing I could just quietly find a seat, but regulations had to be observed, so I said, "Second medical officer on the bridge, sir."

"Andi!" the Captain smiled. "How's your father doing?"

"He's still resting," I said, trying to make my voice sound light and casual, and failing miserably.

He gave me a strange look, but turned back to the fore, only saying, "What are you doing here?"

"I was finished in sickbay, and thought I'd see if I could help out here."

Still preoccupied with the fore view, he gestured to the monitor's station. "Mr. Kane is taking a short break, you might fill in for a moment. There's probably nothing going on, but..."

"Yes sir," I said, as his sentence dwindled into nothingness.

It couldn't hurt. And at the moment, I welcomed any task. Sliding into the chair on the far right of the spacious room, I made sure all the monitors were activated, and proceeded to keep my eye on them for any problem that might pop up in any of the ship's sections.

Even my admittedly untrained eye could see at a glance that all systems were normal, other than the one thruster that was still down and offline. I leaned back in the chair and stole a glance at August, who worked quietly and systematically at the navigations panel.

My brother. The thought rose to the top of my mind, persistently. It was strange to even think the word—but if Commander Howitz were really my father, and I had no doubt of that, then it naturally followed that August was my brother.

What had happened to our mother? Was she still alive? If not, how had she...

A soft beeping started up in front of me, making me come back to the real world. I looked at my station to try to discover the source of it, and saw a red blip on the engineering monitor, blinking away and beeping persistently.

Frowning, I pulled the engineering systems to the main monitor and looked more closely at the blip. It seemed to indicate a power loss to the security systems at the source.

"Captain?" I called, standing.

He was giving an order and didn't hear me. I tried calling louder. "Captain?"

This time, he turned to me. "Yes, what is it?"

For an answer, I pointed to the blip. Then I said, "There seems to be a problem in engineering—I think the security systems."

Crinkling his brow, he stood up and stepped to the monitors. "That's impossible. How could..." He stared at the screen. "You're right. Power loss there... and there!" He pointed to another blip that had just appeared. "Data transfer systems as well. Guilders, slow to propulsion ten."

"Aye sir."

"There was no alert," he mumbled, leaning forward and selecting information on the damage.   "There go the communication systems!"

Another red light popped onto the screen. He pulled up his wristcom, dialed, and began to speak.   "Commander Howitz, what..."

Before he could finish his sentence, the lights on the bridge went out, leaving our faces eerily illuminated by the computer screens and control lights.

CHAPTER XIV

August cried out in surprise as the lights went out, and Guilders spoke more urgently than was his wont. "Captain, we have no warp power."

Swearing under his breath, the Captain groped along the walls until he came to a compartment in the wall and pulled out two electric lanterns. Handing one to me, he said, "Lieutenant, keep a straight course. Mr. Guilders, keep her at high propulsion."

"Yes sir," they said in unison.

"Andi, you'd better get down to sickbay," he urged. "Someone might be hurt."

"Yes sir." Holding the lantern out in front of me, I began slowly making my way through the dark bridge.

When I reached the door, however, it wouldn't open. I started to tell the Captain, when the lights blinked on, and a familiar gravelly voice spoke from the intercom, half obscured by static. "Captain, one side of the main reactor has burned out. I've managed to transfer partial solar power to the lights and communication systems, but the warp, data control subsystems, and security are still down, and it looks like we might be losing shields and thermal control, also."

Gritting his teeth, the Captain dropped into his chair and spoke. "If you can salvage anything, Commander, keep the thermal control running, that's the most important. Why didn't the alert sound?"

"Data transfer went out first. Everything's going to be slow."

I turned off my lantern and said quickly, "Captain, the door..."

After a quick glance at me, he spoke into the intercom on his chair arm again. "Get power to the doors right away, Commander."

"Aye, sir."

"Slow to propulsion five, Mr. Guilders. We can't drain the power any more than necessary."

"Aye, sir."

Order after order was given, and there was an air of tension all through the bridge. In that moment, as I stood waiting by the door, it came to me that the Doctor hadn't called to see if I was all right. Usually, he would have been calling me as soon as there was a problem to see where I was and how I was doing, but my wristcom hadn't so much as beeped since this whole thing started. Was he all right?

I leaned against the door and nearly fell through when it slid open. As I regained my balance, I called, "The doors are working now, Captain!"

Normally I would have received a good-natured laugh in response to this, but he had too much on his mind. "Very well, get down to sickbay immediately."

"Yes sir." I jumped out the doors and hurried through the halls and down the elevator.

Contrary to the Captain's fears, there was no one who needed tending. Often during failures, crewmen would get caught in malfunctioning machinery, or badly bruised and jarred by the bumps and jolts. But not this time. At least not yet.

I felt strangely apprehensive, standing there all alone in the middle of sickbay. Something wasn't right, I could feel it. Something new—it was more than my knee or my father, or any of those problems I'd already been aware of. Something just wasn't right. Power didn't fail without warning and for no reason, and the chance of all one-hundred-twelve crew members remaining uninjured was poor to nonexistent.

The sound of running water from the direction of the sanitation room nearly made me jump out of my skin. I stumbled slightly, then caught myself on the end of one of the cots. Who was in there?

I waited, heart still beating rapidly from the start I'd received. The water shut off, and I felt apprehension as I waited for the whirring, gusty sound of the drier.

It didn't come.

Instead, I heard slow, weary footsteps, and the Doctor appeared in the doorway, his hands and face moist.

My heart pounded fiercely as I stared at him. He stared back, peering, and the confused, almost frightened look on his face as he looked at me almost broke my heart.

"Remind me again of your name?" he said at last, and his voice was utterly lost.

Forgetting about my father, my questions and everything else, I rushed to him and caught his hand in both of mine. It was slippery with lingering water. "It's me, Andi. Don't you know me, Doctor?"

"Andi. Yes." But he didn't look as though he understood. "I think... patients all gone... Trent called..."

"Why can't you remember anything?" I cried, finding I had to say something, *anything* to keep him from going on in that lost manner.

He shook his head sadly. "I don't know what you mean. I'm just so confused. Help me, please." He pulled his hands away and buried his face in them.

"I will. Lay down, I'll do a scan."

"A scan? What kind of scan are you going to do?" His bewildered look remained, but he lay down on the nearest cot submissively.

"I'll use the new CMR scanner. Just stay here, I'll be right back."

Hurrying towards the primary medical cabinet, I opened the drawer where the scanners were supposed to be. The drawer was empty. "Where did you put the new scanner?" I asked.

He sat up slightly. "I don't know what you mean."

Realizing that asking him anything would be useless, I tried to figure out where it might be. Remembering that he had been in the sanitation room just before he'd come into sickbay, I checked there.

There were puddles of water all over the floor and the counter, and one of the sinks was full of water. I drained it, fighting to keep my heart from plummeting, and spotted the scanner laying in a puddle of water nearby. I hastily picked it up and dried it thoroughly, but to my dismay, it wouldn't turn on. I'd have to find the other one.

Looking around the room, I strove to divorce my feelings from my mind. I couldn't worry about the Doctor's condition right now, what I needed to focus on was helping him.

The other scanner didn't appear to be in the room, so I went back out to look around for it. When I got there, I saw that the Doctor had stood up and was taking his jacket off a peg on the wall.

"Doctor, what are you doing? I thought you were going to wait for a scan?"

He looked at me, and I saw with a sense of relief that his expression was normal, although tired. The lost look was gone.

"I'm fine. I just need some rest."

"I'd feel more comfortable if I could just give you a scan, Doctor. It won't take long.

He hung his coat back up. "All right."

I hurried through the otherwise deserted sickbay, looking beside each cot and in each medical cabinet. I finally found it in the personal effects box of one of the stations. This worried me. Clearly, he didn't know what he was doing, which meant he *definitely* shouldn't be treating anyone.

I ran back to him just as he was getting up again. "Doctor, please lay down," I said urgently.

"Why?" Once again, his eyes were bewildered. "I want to

go to my quarters."

I laid my hand firmly on his shoulder, forcing myself to speak professionally. *He's just a patient, just another patient...* "Just let me do a scan quickly, please."

He lay down again, and when I tried to switch the scanner on this time, it worked. I connected it to his monitor and began moving it slowly, a couple of inches away from his head.

Not moving, he stared at the ceiling, a vacant look in his eyes. I kept my eyes on his monitor, looking for anything out of the ordinary.

At first, nothing seemed at all unusual. Everything looked perfectly normal. I was about to move on to another part of the body, when something caught my eye.

I moved the scanner back to the middle of the forehead. There seemed to be a slight movement—a feeble vibration of various regions of the cerebral cortex, including the medial temporal lobe. *Medial temporal lobe...* I struggled to remember its functions. *Long-term memory...*

I looked at the monitor again, and pressed a section of the screen to magnify the image. Yes, definitely an unusual vibration. It was irregular, and spasmodic, and unlike anything I'd ever seen.

I intensified scanner power to seven points, to focus in on his cerebrum. That didn't reveal anything to show me the cause of the vibration.

I glanced at his face. He had closed his eyes, and lay with his hands stiffly at his sides, his face wearing a restless frown.

Focusing the scanner even further, I studied the right cerebral hemisphere closely, looking for any similar movements of the hippocampus, also related to memory. As expected, there was a slight vibration.

I studied the other hemisphere as well, but there was nothing wrong there. The Doctor was left-handed, so his cerebral dominance must be the right hemisphere.

Turning the scanner off, I laid it down and sat slowly on the cot next to his, severely perplexed. What did it mean? Obviously there was something wrong with his memory.

He opened his eyes, and I saw with a sinking heart that he looked even more confused and lost than before. "Can I go now?"

"Yes, I think you'd better get some rest, Doctor."

My heart ached as he nodded mechanically, got up and walked out, leaving his jacket hanging on the wall. He was acting like he either didn't know me, or didn't care anything about me. I longed to run into his arms, to hear his gruff voice reassuring me, to know that he loved me. But he didn't say another word. He just left.

"Goodnight, Doctor," I whispered. Then I bowed my head and tried to make sense of my raging emotions for a moment.

"Andi!"

I stiffened. It was him.

"Yes sir?" Not turning around, I steeled myself for anything. This emotional roller coaster was getting to be too much for me.

Footsteps rushed towards me, and I turned in surprise. His face was intelligent, though his forehead was lined and the circles under his eyes were as dark and long as before. He caught up my left hand and gripped it in both his. "Andi!"

"What? What is it?" I cried. What did he have to say? Something about Langham's Disease and my past? His memory loss?

"You... you..." A shadow swept over his face, blotting out the assurance, and he blinked at me, the spark of intellect in his eyes dulling rapidly. "You... can't."

"Can't what? What can't I do?"

He looked down at me, confusion and clarity struggling on his face. "You can't—something about—Emmett. No—Erasmus."

Erasmus. Howitz. My father.

"What about Erasmus?" I asked, trying to keep my voice from rising.

"You can't."

"Can't *what*?" I cried.

"Erasmus—you can't. We need it!"

Cold washed over my heart. He was telling me not to go with my father, not to let him help me. Could my father be right? Could he—want to keep me for himself—want the radialloy for himself?

Feeling like crying, I reached my free hand towards the command button on my wristcom.

With a wild cry, the Doctor caught my wrist, gripping it hard. "Don't... listen! You can't do this."

His eyes were wider than I'd ever seen. As I stared into them, I saw an empty darkness that I didn't recognize.

I pulled my other wrist up to my face and jammed my chin on the button before he could stop me. I forced out the words, trying not to choke on them. "Captain Trent, I'm—sorry to report that I have found—Doctor Lloyd unfit for duty."

CHAPTER XV

We just stared for a moment, then I whispered, "I'm sorry, Doctor."

He let go of me abruptly, just as the Captain's voice answered. "If you're sure, Andi. I've sent security. Let me know the details later."

He trusted me. I'd just told him that his best friend was unfit for his lifelong work, and he believed me without question. I felt dazed, and helpless. This was a nightmare.

The Doctor just dropped to the cot opposite me and stared, his eyes still wide, but saying nothing. I tried to speak, failed, and then jumped up, turned, and fled.

At first I didn't know where I was running, but before long I found that my legs were taking me to engineering, a place I'd been only twice, both times when the ship was in spacedock. I had to talk with my father. I had no one to turn to right now, no one knew what had been happening except him, and I couldn't tell anyone else. These problems were my own, the Captain, Guilders, and Almira, the only people I would have trusted enough to talk to about it, were all too busy. They had to worry about the ship, not my personal family struggles.

When I was safe inside the elevator, I dared to breath, gasping in a lungful of oxygen before saying, "E-Deck," and letting myself be carried down.

I took deep breaths as I moved down the ship, focusing intently on the indicator lights all around the tiny room.

God... oh God! I tried to pray, but had no words. *What's happening? The Doctor... my father... the radialloy... what are you doing?* I'd always been told that He knew what He was doing, that He had a plan. That all things would work together for good. *How can anything ever be good again?* Had He made a mistake?

The elevator doors opened out onto E-Deck, and I hesitated before stepping out. It was highly unlikely that the radiation would do anything to my knee. I wouldn't stay long.

I put my boot forward and placed it onto the smooth metal floor in front of me, then began walking resolutely forward.

The large, octagonal room was empty. I looked around at each station, but no one occupied them. The giant reactor in the middle glowed faintly, and I saw a makeshift aluminum plate covering an area that I assumed was the hole.

I frowned at the silence, but walked forward, my boots ticking on the floor with each cautious step. Once again, something just wasn't right. True, I'd never visited engineering when it was in operation, but I'd heard the Captain call down there from the bridge. Every time, there had been sounds of talking and general working in the background. Now, it was too quiet.

I stopped about a yard from the reactor, hesitating to approach it. As I stood, unsure what to do, I heard a faint voice from somewhere ahead. It was low and gravelly.

My heart rose in my throat, but I sidestepped the reactor and tip-toed in the direction of the voice. It became clearer as I approached, and when I'd come about two feet from a metal door labeled "Fission Control Chamber," I could make out the words.

Commander Howitz was speaking with controlled determination. "I'm not sure, but I'll need at least a few days. It must not be repaired before then."

Another voice grumbled. "You still haven't explained why this is so important."

When the Commander's voice answered, it was harsh. "It's important to *you* because if you don't comply, there will be consequences. If you do, there will be rewards. That is all that matters."

A youthful cry broke in. "What are you talking about? What is this?"

"How did you get in here? Who are you?"

"He's a thruster repair man..."

"Hurry, get him, men! He'll tell Trent! You know what that will mean for everyone!"

There was a rush of boots towards the door, and I whirled on my heel and ran, ran for all I was worth, back towards the elevator. The metal floor was slippery, and I couldn't seem to move quickly enough.

When I reached the elevator, I pounded the button, praying for it to come quickly.

Before it did, a door behind me burst open, and I turned to look over my shoulder. It was the door to Fission Control, and crewmen spilled out of it. In front, running, was a young man, younger than myself, his eyes wide with fear. The eyes met mine just before he was grabbed from behind and pulled back. Out of the crowd, I saw Commander Howitz's dark eyes, staring at me. I didn't move—I couldn't think. I couldn't understand the expression on his face—it was somehow dark and seemed forbidding, and yet sorry. He started towards me, and I heard his voice rise commandingly out of the chaos, but I couldn't understand his words.

As the elevator door finally opened, I heard a sharp cry of pain, which seemed to unlock my muscles. I jumped in and almost screamed, "A-Deck!"

The Commander bounded forward, calling to the others. I let out another scream as he came nearer, but the doors closed in his face and I was sped upwards.

He was an engineer. He'd try to stop me. Heart racing, I called, "Cancel. D-Deck." A second later, the elevator stopped, and the doors began opening. When they were halfway open, they died, leaving a space just barely wide enough for me. I squeezed through and rushed across to the other elevator on the other side of the corridor. "A-Deck," I instructed, adrenaline pumping. It pulled me upwards.

I leaned impatiently against the door when it stopped, and nearly tumbled out when they slid open, revealing the short A-Deck hall. Righting myself, I rushed towards the bridge, feeling like I wasn't getting any nearer.

At last I reached the doors and they slid open. Not waiting to use the proper protocol, I yelled, "Sabotage!"

Silence reigned. The Captain swiveled his chair to look up at me, his eyebrows raised. Everyone else turned to me, too, with looks of mingled surprise and expectation on their faces.

"It's sabotage," I said, forcing myself to speak calmly and coherently, yet still with a thread of urgency. "The power failure—Commander Howitz did it. I just heard him talking to the mates and engineers."

The Captain's eyebrows lowered. "What's going on, Andi? You call me to say your father is unfit for duty, and then when I come down to talk to you about it, you're gone. Now you come rushing in here..."

"There's no time to explain!" I cried, jumping down the few steps into the command pit and gripping the arm of his chair. "Something's happened to the Doctor... I don't know what, but something's wrong with him. And Commander Howitz sabotaged the reactor. I don't know why, but he did."

I remembered Peat and Sigmet's claim that they'd come to arrest Commander Howitz, and how they had to wait for the ship to get back in communication range so it could be verified. Could he have performed the sabotage so that the ship wouldn't reach that point? Did he really have something to hide?

That possibility had probably already occurred to the Captain. He jumped up and began speaking. "Mr. Guilders, slow to propulsion zero. Mr. Ralston, shut down automation immediately, go to all manual. Andi, you're sure about this?"

"Yes sir. He knows I heard him, he'll be up any minute..."

"Ralston, seal doors immediately."

"It'll be a minute sir."

"Mr. Yanendale, contact the *Alacrity I* and inform them that we are..."

The door at the back of the bridge burst open, and I jumped, letting go of the Captain's chair like a guilty child caught in the sweets.

There stood Commander Howitz, a charged blaster in his hand. Behind him were some men—I couldn't tell how many—also with blasters. The Commander's face was set and hard, and he looked at the Captain, not at me.

"There will be no messages sent, Captain Trent." His low, gravelly voice seemed to fill the bridge somehow, settling in every corner.

A creak made me turn my head, and I saw Mr. Yanendale leaning forward urgently to press a button. I couldn't see what button, but I guessed that he was sending out an "emergency" message, so that the *Alacrity* or any other nearby vessel would receive it and get word that we were in trouble.

Commander Howitz saw him, too. Before Yanendale's finger could come down on the button, the Commander had fired, and a blast of energy spurted from the gun and hit the comm marshal in the chest.

I screamed, the Captain leapt forward, and Yanendale gasped and fell back. I jumped off of the command platform to help him, but the Commander's voice barked at me, "Stay back."

Blindly, I kept going forward for a moment, but the Captain grabbed my arm and yanked me back, clutching me to him. I felt his chest moving quickly in and out.

No one moved. The Commander turned his weapon back on the Captain and myself.

"Over by the fore window," he ordered, beckoning with the blaster. "A single line."

The Captain let go of me, and I followed Guilders out of the command pit. August didn't move from his seat, but he stared at his father with wide eyes, and the color had drained from his face. That worried me.

"Quickly!"

We lined up: myself, the Captain, Ralston, and the gunner and monitor.

"Martin," the Commander ordered. "If any of them have weapons, take them."

Mr. Martin, an engine technician, stepped out from behind him and advanced. Mr. Yanendale groaned.

"Dad," August began, but the Commander shot him a warning glare. August was silent.

Martin walked down the row, checking for weapons. He took them from the Captain and Guilders, not changing his expression one iota.

"Is this mutiny, Commander Howitz?" the Captain fumed.

"Indeed it is, Captain Trent." He beckoned for Martin to take the weapons away. "Or it will be, unless you cooperate."

"In what way?"

I kept my eyes trained on August. He was paler than ever, and his mouth was slightly open as he stared at his father. I didn't know if it was open because he was shocked or if he might start hyperventilating, but I watched him just in case.

"I would like to be taken to my speeder, which has been programmed to autopilot and wait for me in sector four-thousand. Orbit five, the Demeter system."

"Not so fast, Howitz," came a deep voice from behind him.

I nearly fell over as Peat and Sigmet stepped out from behind him. They had caught him! But—why hadn't he seen to it that they were in the brig, or otherwise taken care of? What was he doing, anyway? Was he really a criminal? My head spun.

"What do you mean?" asked the Commander, not lowering his weapon or taking his eyes off of us.

"We had an agreement," Sigmet spoke up, his high eyes suspicious.

"I had to act earlier than planned," Commander Howitz assured, just looking over his shoulder for an instant before turning back to us. "Circumstances made it necessary."

Peat grumbled, but Sigmet nodded, his eyes narrowed.

"Wait!" I cried. "I thought you said he was a criminal and you were here to catch him?"

"Andi." The Captain put his arm out in front of me. I fell silent.

"Our reasons are our own," said Peat haughtily. "We will take care of him in our own way."

They left, casting a glance at the Commander before walking out.

"You can't be serious about this, Howitz," the Captain said.

"I am."

"And if I refuse?"

"First of all, you'll be sent to the brig along with anyone else who gets in the way. Secondly, it might interest you to know that if we don't get to my speeder in twenty hours—by twelve o' clock tomorrow—your friend Doctor Lloyd will be permanently insane."

I felt him stiffen beside me, but I was too shocked to take notice of this. What? What did he mean? What was he—did he have anything to do with—

"Dad, you promised!" August cried, standing up.

"Sit *down*, August, or I'll have you up here with the rest of them," the Commander ordered.

August didn't sit down, but he paled until he was nearly white.

I looked pleadingly at the Captain. I didn't care what was going on here. We couldn't let the Doctor go insane. He had to be all right.

"All you want is to get to your speeder in less than twenty hours?" the Captain said slowly.

"I want that, and I want my daughter."

"Your... what?" the Captain cried.

I gulped. My brain wasn't working... I was too stunned—I tried to sort out the situation. The Commander had come aboard looking for me, and somehow, somehow, he had found me, and now wanted me back with him. He wanted me so badly that he'd take me by force, mutiny, sabotage—anything it took.

There was only one reason for this that I could think of—he had lied to me. He wanted the radialloy as much as Peat and Sigmet had. Realizing that they had put me on my guard by both speaking to me as they had, they'd agreed to work together, probably planning to cut each other out at some point.

"This young lady is my daughter," the Commander informed, pointing his weapon at me. "When I leave, she goes with me."

August cried out, and when I turned to look, he swayed, tried to clutch at the navigation panel, and then dropped to the deck.

CHAPTER XVI

I darted towards August with a cry, and this time I wasn't corrected by either the Captain or my father. I felt over his head, where a bump was already forming, and then grasped for his wrist while I studied his breathing.

"Well, Captain?" Commander Howitz went on. "Time is wasting."

"Andi?" the Captain said in a low voice.

Feeling August's skin, I found it to be cold and clammy. His blood pressure must have dropped, making him go into shock. Now the Captain was asking if I would cooperate—I had to. It was all we could do for now, it seemed. Perhaps later we could find a way to save the Doctor ourselves.

I turned back towards where he stood by the fore window, eyeing me. I nodded.

"I will do as you ask," he said through clenched teeth. "On the condition that you do not harm Doctor Lloyd."

Commander Howitz made no verbal reply, and I had turned back to August, so I couldn't see if he made any sign of agreement. August's breathing was quick and shallow, and his pulse was feeble and accelerated. Urgency showed through my tones as I spoke up. "Commander, he needs to get to sickbay."

When I turned to look at him, I found I could not read his face at all. It was like a mask. "Jarvis, carry him down there. Then you may return for Mr. Yanendale."

The crewman he addressed walked over and hoisted August up in his arms, then waited, apparently for me to lead the way off the bridge. I did so, my brain whirling with all that had happened. But no. I couldn't get overwhelmed. My brother needed me.

And he was not the only one, I realized when I reached sickbay. Someone else was already there, a young man, who'd been dumped on the cot nearest the door, and now lay fighting back groans, with beads of sweat standing on his face.

"Put him over there," I ordered, finding that my voice shook frustratingly as I pointed to another cot.

Jarvis obeyed, laying August down gently. Then he turned and went back out.

I longed to go take care of August, but knew that I must have a look at the other young crewman first. From where I stood by the doorway, I could not see the extent of his injuries, but they must be very painful.

Unbuttoning my jacket on the way over to his cot, I tossed it behind me. I'd pick it up later, and I didn't have time just now to grab a medical tunic either. My white shirt would have to do.

Maybe the Captain was right... maybe we do need a nurse.

But we wouldn't need one, if the Doctor would just get better. What had Commander Howitz meant when he said...

No. No matter how difficult it was, I had to calm myself and work professionally. I said a small prayer, took a deep breath, and stepped beside the young man's cot.

It was the same fellow I'd seen down in engineering, the one who'd been chased out the door. A young mate, and the unnatural angle of his arm told me there was probably a subluxation of the humerus.

He was probably a couple of years younger than myself, and with his eyes closed, his face shining with perspiration, and his hair falling over his eyes he looked so pitiful that I felt like crying. But I scolded myself again and laid a finger gently on his shoulder.

His eyes flew open, and a grunt of pain escaped his determined lips.

I forced my voice to steady. "Your shoulder is dislocated.

I'll take care of it."

I reached into the closest medical cabinet for a local anesthetic.

"Did you warn him?" he asked, through tightly closed teeth.

"Not in time," I sighed, filling a hypo with the drug.

His left fist clenched, while the fingers of the right moved slightly. He groaned again.

"Don't try to move," I urged, picking up a pair of scissors and walking around to the other side of the cot. Normally his shirt and jacket would be removed, but I'd seen easily that that would be out of the question. It would be too damaging to the shoulder, so I'd just have to cut the right sleeve of both off. His jacket was rumpled and torn—he'd have to get a new one anyway.

After that was done, I injected the anesthetic and waited for a minute.

"What happened down there?" I asked.

As he answered, his voice was strained. "I had just come in—for a report—on the broken thruster. Didn't know at first—what was going on. Guess—I shouldn't have let them know that I wasn't one of them."

"Did they do this?" I asked, touching his arm and preparing to begin reduction of the injured joint.

He barely nodded his head. "I was—the only one—they were trying to get me—help them but—I'll always be—on the Captain's— side."

I gritted my teeth as I worked, trying to keep tears from filling my eyes. It was so heartbreaking—some mother somewhere had reason to be proud of this boy.

He gripped the sheets as I carefully and precisely moved the bone back into its socket, then felt the muscles around the joint to ensure that everything was correctly placed. Then when I laid the arm back down, he breathed out a sigh.

"Thank you," he said.

"What's your name?" I asked.

"Kerwin Merritt," he said.

"Well, Kerwin Merritt, you'll need to rest here for a few hours," I instructed, preparing a sedative. "This will help you relax."

He nodded again, and his "Thanks" was nearly in a whisper.

After I'd administered the drug, I looked down at him one last time, and then slipped away to the other side of the room, where August lay.

His eyes were still closed, but some color had come back into his face so that he no longer looked like a breathing corpse. His breathing, though still rather shallow, had slowed some, and as I approached, I could see that his face was pinched, as if he were having a bad dream.

"August?" I said softly, laying a hand on his arm.

I hadn't expected him to open his eyes, but he did, and they stared up into mine with deep astonishment. For a moment, neither of us spoke.

"You," he said at last in a disbelieving voice. "You are Genevieve?"

I shook my head as suppressed emotions poured over me, leaving me utterly exhausted. "My name is Andi. Andi, and I don't ever want to be called anything else!" I sank onto the cot opposite him and wept.

Another moment of silence, and then he said, "But... but my father said you were dead."

I shook my head, unable to speak. Then, I asked the question that had been plaguing me somewhere deep inside ever since my father had made his revelation. "Did my mother—our mother—die in childbirth? Did *I* kill her?"

"No!" his answer was definite, and more stern that anything I'd heard from him.

Raising my head, I asked, "Then how did she die?"

He raised himself on one elbow and shook his head sadly. "I don't know. I was only five. She disappeared the same time as you, that's all I know. My father said you were both dead."

A light came on in my mind. "She's the one who took me to

the Doctor," I sniffed. That had to be it. She'd seen, somehow, that I was not safe, and had taken me to the Doctor. Why would she take me to *him*? He hadn't seemed to know my father.

"How did he find me?" I asked.

He shook his head, the dazed look still in his eyes, and sat up slowly, never taking his eyes off me. "I don't know. I never even knew until today that you were—alive."

I couldn't speak. The enormous lump in my throat prohibited it, so I gave up trying and kept on sobbing.

After a long moment, he stood up, took the few steps to me hesitantly, then, more hesitating still, he took my hands and lifted me up. Then he put his arms around me and held me close.

I cried on his shoulder, wishing he would hold me tighter, but glad that he had taken initiative to embrace me as his sister, his family. With the Doctor acting stranger all the time, and my real father having betrayed me, August was the only family I had right now.

When I had quieted somewhat, he spoke softly and seriously.

"Dad told me that he'd just come here looking for a job."

"Why here?" I asked, pulling back and pushing my hair out of my eyes.

"He has a device to help him locate nuclear power sources with electrostatic ion thrusters, which is his specialty."

Something didn't seem right about that, but I couldn't put my finger on it. "I don't understand..." I began, but when I looked up at August's face, I saw that the color had drained from it again.

"What?" I cried.

He shook his head, and his Adam's apple moved as he swallowed. "I almost forgot... your father... I mean, Doctor Lloyd."

"What about him?" I asked, my calm fleeing from me.

"Has he been acting strange—crazy—for a few days?"

"Yes. I scanned him—there must be something wrong with his memory." I explained about the scan I'd done, and what I'd seen.

He turned from me, and I saw his hands begin shaking. "Did you say—vibration? Was it sporadic? Irregular?"

"Yes."

He appeared to be holding his breath. "And—does he have an unusual obsession with washing his face and hands?"

My mind went back to his dripping face and hands, and the puddles of water in the sanitation room. "Yes... yes he does."

"No," he whispered. "I knew it, but—he promised!" He pounded a white fist on the wall, and his dark eyes expressed anger I hadn't expected from him.

"What is it?" I gasped.

He looked back at me. "I know what's wrong with him."

"What? *What?*"

"My father," he began, "—our father—is an inventor. Some call him a genius. Some call him a monster. He brought many of his inventions on the ship when we signed up. Like the device I told you about."

He paused, and I pleaded with him to continue.

"One of the machines he brought... he—he calls it his memory eradicator."

CHAPTER XVII

My mind reeled. "Memory... eradicator? What does that do?"

He spoke even more quickly. "He used to use it on his adversaries. It locks by x-ray to the portions of the brain related to memory and transmits disturbing electrical impulses. The impulses displace stored images, and cause the subject to confuse short and long term memories. It works over a period of time to..."

I couldn't listen to any more. I clapped my hand over my mouth to stifle a scream, feeling like I was going to be sick. August jerked his shoulders back.

"The process is reversible up to a certain point. My dad said twenty hours. That's until he goes insane. After that, if he's not taken care of in another twenty-four—he'll die."

It all came together in my head. "That's what happened to Doctor Holmes."

"Who?"

I grabbed his arm. "When Crash came, he said that he'd talked to Doctor Holmes on Earth, and he was barely lucid. He died the next day. He told Crash to warn the Doctor."

"You mean Dad... used it to get this doctor to tell him where you were?"

I nodded. "He must have. And then—" I thought quickly, feeling my mind suddenly clear and begin to race. "When Crash heard about two scientists leaving Earth, he thought that was the threat. They were chasing after Commander Howitz—father—trying to get to the radialloy before he did."

"The what?" he looked utterly lost. He must not have heard about the radialloy.

"Do you think he really means he'll let the Doctor go insane if we don't reach your speeder in time?"

August's face grew angry. "Not only that, but I don't believe he'll stop it even if we do get there in time."

"August, we have to save him! You have to stop it!"

"I can't!" he cried back. "Even if I knew how, I couldn't get to the machine! He has it locked in his quarters."

My mind kept racing, grasping after a solution. There had to be one. There had to be one somewhere. "We have to contact Crash and Whales and get them to help."

"But how? There's no way to transmit—he's taken communications offline."

"Maybe we can get it back—or divert power from something else."

"He'd be sure to notice. Don't underestimate him, Andi."

I backed up a step, angry. "I'm not just going to stand here and do nothing! There has to be a way."

Before he could respond, a voice from the door startled us. "Lieutenant Howitz, your father orders you to return to the bridge immediately. We're making the warp jump."

August looked down at me with a sorrowful expression. "I wish I could help you. But I can't."

Hot tears stung my eyes, overflowing, draining the hope out of me. I looked at him pleadingly, but he turned and followed the officer out.

I wanted to drop to the cot and cry again, but just as they left the room, Mr. Jarvis came back in with Mr. Yanendale, the com marshal. I didn't know what had delayed him, and I didn't want to. I just needed to focus on my work right now.

Taking a breath so deep I could feel the oxygen spreading to every cell, I approached the cot where he lay, his narrow face chalky and pained. Mr. Jarvis looked sternly at me.

"He is to be taken to the brig as soon as you have finished

treating him," the officer said brusquely, then seated himself watchfully on the other side of the room.

Blood covered the patient's left shoulder, staining his uniform. So the blast hadn't hit his chest, as I first thought. Still, it was a nasty wound, and they'd taken their own sweet time in getting him down here. The hole in his jacket was charred around the edges, indicative of blaster fire. I steeled myself. I'd dealt with things like this before, and hadn't been bothered. It was just that my nerves had been worn nearly raw by the events of the day.

Carefully, gently, I pried the jacket away from the wound and slid the sleeve off his arm. "Did you manage to send a message?" I whispered hopefully.

In the same cautious tone, he replied, "I don't think so. I pushed the button when he wasn't looking, but nothing happened. I think communications—had already been—taken offline." He moaned a bit as I pulled his shirt away from the bloody wound.

"How bad is it?" he asked faintly.

I sighed. "A ruptured artery, and some muscle damage. I can repair it, but you'll need to wear the arm in a sling for awhile, to minimize movement until it finishes healing, and it will be sore for quite awhile." I pressed a pad of sterile dressing to the wound to slow the bleeding while I got the regen ready.

After I'd finished repairing the wound, I carefully sat him up and slung the arm close to his chest, adjusting the strap so that it wouldn't move too much. When I had at last finished, I looked at him. He looked back and tried to smile.

"He said you have to go to the brig."

"I know."

With a glance at his pale face, I beckoned to the guard, who sat sternly in the corner, to indicate that he could take the patient away now. With little ceremony, he escorted Mr. Yanendale from the room.

Exhausted, I sank into a chair in the corner closest to the door. My mind was too tired to think anymore. I had to rest for a few minutes—

Why. Why was my father so intent on having the radialloy? And *how*? How had he found me?

First I sorted out the stories I'd been told by him and by Peat and Sigmet. I decided to believe his story of what the radialloy was, since he'd proved that I did have Langham's disease. The only part I discarded, for the moment anyway, was the idea that there was another cure. I no longer believed that he wanted to save me.

Then I put Crash's story together with August's and came up with an imperfect idea of what had happened in the past. My mother had taken me to the Doctor, dying before she could return home. Perhaps my father had planned to take the radialloy away from me, to sell it, and she'd wanted to save me? This didn't make total sense, but I accepted it for the moment.

Several years later, after I'd been raised by the Doctor and gone to space, my father had for some reason decided he needed to find the radialloy again. Possibly he'd gotten in trouble with someone and needed the money or the radialloy itself to get out of it. Perhaps he'd worked with Peat and Sigmet, and they needed it. Or maybe their supervisor did, and he'd sent them after it. They must be the two scientists—Leeke and his assistant Mars that Crash had mentioned. Regardless, my father had picked up August and come after me, after tracking me to Grand Forks, seeking out the Doctor's closest friend—Doctor Holmes—and finding out from him that we'd gone to space.

One thing still didn't make any sense at all—how? How had he tracked me here?

Impulsively, I stood up and walked over to where I'd left the CMR scanner the night before. What if this whole thing was a mistake, and I didn't really have the radialloy after all? It was high time I made sure.

Seating myself on one of the cots, I plugged the scanner into the adjacent monitor and turned it on. I hesitated for one moment.. The Doctor had said never to use it on myself, because the magnet could pull at my implant. But I'd just use it for a second. Not allowing myself time to think more about it, I pulled my skirt above my legging-clad right knee, set the scanner to one point, and moved it above my leg.

For an instant, my mind focused on the image displayed on the monitor. The patella was visible, but was most definitely not all bone. That was evident at a glance. There was metal in the middle of it, just as the Doctor had told me, though the scanner couldn't identify what kind.

Then it was true—

Scarcely had I taken all this in, when my knee grew suddenly hot. The heat intensified rapidly, and a familiar spasm shot through my knee. With a cry of pain, I had the presence of mind to shut the scanner off. The pain dropped almost as rapidly as it had arisen, again leaving a numb, warm throbbing.

CHAPTER XVIII

Shaken from the experience and the horrible memories it brought, I fell back on the cot, breathing hard. Just like on the bridge.

Then, in one quick motion, I sat straight up. The bridge.

"...he has a device to help locate nuclear power sources with electrostatic ion thrusters..."

The *Surveyor* didn't have electrostatic ion thrusters, did she. She had ionized plasma thrusters, I remembered now.

So he had been lying to August. That wasn't what the device was for. But the device must have led him here. And August was no fool—whatever his father told him would have to be close enough to the truth to seem plausible.

The CMR scanner! Compact magnetic resonance scanner. Magnetic resonance imaging. I knew that a few hundred years ago an MRI had filled up a whole room. Even when the Doctor was in medical school, they had been enormous, to accommodate the size of the magnet required. But now, they were small. A method had been developed to strengthen the magnet using safe radiation.

Dozens of facts flooded my mind. The twinges in my knee, that I'd thought nothing of at the time, had occurred less than a week before August and his father arrived. The intense, unbearable pain on the bridge—

My mind rushed back to that day. For the first second after I hit the ground I felt shaken, but normal. Then the pain arose suddenly, just like with the scan, and continued for several seconds before stopping rather abruptly, just as when I'd shut off the scanner. August had been resting in the quarters he shared with his father, and had later told me that many of his father's devices had been thrown around by the impact, and he'd had to get up and take care of it.

Of course. The device that had led him here could detect the radialloy. The twinges—those had been brought on as he sought to ascertain where I was. And when we'd hit the asteroid, it had fallen and been accidentally turned on, and the close proximity of it had let off such radiation that it had resulted in greatly intensified pain. When August turned it off—not knowing what it really was—the radiation had abated, and the pain had subsided.

I no longer had any doubt that it was the radialloy that my father wanted—not me.

I should have told the Captain about everything long before, then we wouldn't be in this trouble now. The Captain had never let me down, and was trustworthy.

Just like the Doctor.

I had to help him. I had to tell the Doctor I was sorry, and pay for my mistake. I had to fix everything, back how it was before.

Just as I was about to head out the door to find the Doctor, an officer stepped in, his face stern.

"Miss Lloyd, dinner is served."

My heart sank. Commander Howitz knew just where I was, and meant to ensure that I went to dinner. But it didn't matter. Somehow, I would outsmart him, and save my father. My real father—the one who had the best right to my trust, love, and loyalty.

* * *

The Captain, Guilders, August, and the other primary bridge officers sat together at a table in one corner of the mess hall, along with myself. I looked around anxiously for the Doctor, but he was nowhere to be seen.

Armed guards stood in the far corners of the room, alert,

and primarily focused on our little group.

The Captain was seething, and it was all Guilders could do to contain him.

"The villain." He tore a bite out of his steak. "The audacity of that..."

"Calm yourself, Harrison," said Guilders calmly. It was the first time I'd ever heard him use the Captain's first name. I wasn't sure what he expected to accomplish with that. "If they hear you talking that way, they'll only keep a closer watch on us."

It didn't seem to have much of an effect on the Captain. He muttered, "Well what are we going to do about it? I'm not just going to sit here and let him take my command." He glared at Commander Howitz, wrath shooting from his eyes. "He's blocked my wristcom from transmitting. He says he'll do the same to anyone who causes trouble."

Curious, I entered the Doctor's com number and tried to call. Nothing.

I kept quiet and focused on eating. August, too, stayed out of the discussion.

"For now, we shall have to do as he says," Guilders observed.

"You're no help at all," the Captain spluttered, then looked suspiciously at August. "And what are you doing here? Did your father send you to spy on us?"

August maintained his silence.

"There has to be some way we can get the ship back."

"Careful, Captain," I ventured. "If we aren't careful, he might hurt the Doctor."

"What is all that about, anyway? I don't understand. How does he know Gerry will go insane?"

I choked, and let my eyes plead with August. He quietly explained about the machine, while I picked at my food, appetite suddenly gone.

The other men were quiet when he had finished. The Captain looked at me. "Why would he do that?"

"I don't know," I managed. "I think—he just wanted a hostage." I also thought that he hadn't wanted me to be able to consult the Doctor, but I kept quiet about that. I still wasn't sure who to trust—there were three other men at the table besides the Captain and Guilders. Sure they'd worked there a long time, but who knew beyond doubt which side they were on?

"Where is the machine now?" the Captain asked.

"He's locked it in his quarters," August answered.

"As Captain, I can override all security systems."

"Could," Guilders pointed out.

August nodded. "He's overridden your clearance. No one can override but him."

"How did he do that?"

August shrugged. His father wasn't informing him about everything, I supposed. After all, he'd made it pretty clear that he didn't agree with the mutiny. I doubted Commander Howitz would turn to him.

The Captain muttered something I couldn't understand, and wasn't sure I wanted to.

"Do you have a plan, Guilders?" I asked hopefully.

The helmsman spoke stoically as he took a bite of his food. "It's much easier to do something without being noticed if one is invisible."

"Invisibility? And just how do you plan to accomplish that?"

Ignoring the Captain's interjection, I asked Guilders, "You mean not draw any attention to yourself? So he won't think of you as a threat?"

"Precisely."

"Does anyone know where the Doctor is?" I asked.

The men all shook their heads. "He's not in his quarters?" the Captain asked, brows furrowing in worry.

"No sir. I checked there on my way to the mess hall. I haven't seen him all day."

The Captain reached out and touched my hand. "We'll save

him, Andi. I promise."

I wasn't reassured. But I tried to sound brave. "Does anyone know how Almira's doing?"

Mr. Ralston, the data controller, spoke up. "I carried a tray into the galley just a moment ago, and saw her. She seemed fine."

I tried to think. If we could contact Crash for help, we'd be well on our way to getting out of this whole horrible mess.

"Captain," I began, leaning forward, but before I could go further, Commander Howitz approached. I jerked back in my chair, hitting my shin on the table leg. I winced, but didn't say anything.

"Hello, Andi," he said with a smile.

I had to fight to keep from grimacing. Did he really think that I was still going to believe him? "Hello."

"I would like to see you in engineering." He said it politely, so politely, that he almost reminded me of August for a moment. But it was a dark politeness, while August's was always soft and rather timid.

"I can't go in engineering," I reminded, sounding more haughty than I intended.

"Did it hurt you before?"

I blushed. "I'll be right down," I said reluctantly.

"Excellent," he smiled. Then his expression turned to a stone that matched the gravelly voice much better as he surveyed the men at the table. "Back to your stations please, gentlemen."

August flushed, and the Captain looked furious, but he knew as well as Guilders that there was nothing they could do, as much as he might rail and complain. All six men stood up, glanced at me, and left.

"Be down in five minutes," he said, trying to soften his face but not exactly succeeding. I nodded, then watched his broad back as he turned and left the mess hall.

CHAPTER XIX

After clearing the table where I'd eaten, and washing my hands, I started down to engineering, butterflies forming in my stomach. The closer I got, the more they fluttered, until I felt like I was going to be sick. I felt as though I were walking directly into a trap, but since I was already in a giant trap, it couldn't possibly make much difference.

As I passed down C-Deck on my way to the elevator, a cabin door slid open as I passed it. I turned to look, and stifled a gasp as I saw Sigmet's odd face peer out at me.

"Come inside," he whispered. "We need to tell you something."

"No," I said, hoping I sounded firm, and prepared to quicken my pace. But he grabbed my arm as I tried to pass. I opened my mouth to scream, but he spoke urgently. "Please, it's in your best interest."

"You can talk to me out here," I insisted. They weren't going to get me to voluntarily become a hostage or whatever they wanted from me.

"Oh, whatever," he said, as Peat stepped out. "There's not much time—he'll find out we're talking to you in about two minutes."

I crossed my arms and planted my feet firmly apart, feeling small and vulnerable beside the muscular Peat. "I know you're not ILA agents. And I know your real names."

"What are they?" Sigmet smiled.

"You're Leeke and Mars, scientists." I forced my voice to

sound accusing.

"Smart girl," Peat nodded, his firm chin looking firmer than ever. "Want to prove how smart you are?"

I didn't know how to answer this, but I didn't need to, because he hurried on. "We weren't lying about Erasmus Sandison. Oh, I know you know him as Erasmus Howitz. He changed his name to keep himself safe. He has a hundred enemies. People he's cheated with his inventions. He's like a con-man—except he never does anything against the law. So he can't be caught—legally.

"But listen to us, Miss Lloyd—he doesn't want to help you. I think you know that now. Father or not, he doesn't care anything about saving your life. But if you come with us—come away from here—we can help you. We'll take you back to our boss and we'll study the radialloy. We'll see if we can find a way to duplicate it, study it to see if we can find an alternate cure. We won't take it until we can make sure you'll be safe."

"Time's up," urged Sigmet.

Peat gripped my shoulder, so hard that I couldn't help wincing, looked me straight in the eyes with an intensity that shriveled me, then gave me a little push down the hall. "Go talk to him now. But don't forget what we've said. Any moment of the day or night you can come to us and we'll manage to get away."

His voice chased after me as I ran towards the elevator, pulse thumping in my ears. I realized when he used the word "manage" why they hadn't taken me already. Their craft was moored, and couldn't get away without clearance—before from the Captain, and now from Commander Howitz.

No, I didn't trust them. For one thing, I knew that Crash distrusted them so much, he'd taken their departure from Earth as a sign of danger to the Doctor. Second, I had no reason to trust them. They wanted the radialloy, and I stood in the way. Why should they protect me? And finally, Peat's intense eyes and Sigmet's odd, shifty, high ones did not inspire the least feeling of safety in me. They never had.

I gritted my teeth as I stepped into the elevator. The flutter in my stomach was gone now. I no longer felt particular curiosity or apprehension about what the Commander wanted to say to me. It wasn't difficult to guess that he wanted to do the same thing Peat and Sigmet had just tried to do—undermine the word of his co-mutineers and try to beat them to the prize.

I was right. When I reached engineering he smiled at me, talked about how much he wanted to save me from them, how teaming up with them had been his only choice, since he had no way to get me away from here. How once we reached his speeder, he and August and I would ride off back to Earth and live happily ever after, and he would keep me safe from all who would harm me. He would take me away now, except that he couldn't override the security on Peat and Sigmet's speeder.

That, I believed. I didn't trust him any more than I'd trusted them. And they, too, were telling the truth in one respect—he had no intention of trying to save me, once he had what he wanted. As he talked I tried to figure out why he didn't just take it out here, but then I realized—the same reason Peat and Sigmet couldn't. They were watching each other too closely. I felt like sighing and smiling at the same time. It was both helpful and horrible to have two sets of villains after me. Honestly, I would almost be amused if it weren't for the fact that my life and the Doctor's sanity were in danger, and one of the villains was my father.

There was no reason to act like I didn't believe him now. I had never had a good poker face, but I pulled on every bit of deceptive or acting power in me to sound trusting. "Thank you. This is all so—scary." I threw in a shudder. The shudder was convincing enough, when I thought about the Doctor. I wanted, longed to ask why the Commander had used the machine on him, but I couldn't. That would only show that I didn't trust him, and right now, that wasn't the best idea.

He smiled, a smile I'd come to hate, and nodded. "I wish you didn't have to go through this."

"I'm tired," I said, feeling like I was going to scream if I had to talk to him another minute. Besides, we only had less than twenty hours to save the Doctor.

With another smile, he reached out his arms to me. Inwardly I shrank back and screamed, but outwardly I hugged him, not tightly, and not long, but I managed to do it. Then I couldn't help turning quickly and rushing back to the elevator.

"Goodnight!" he called after me.

His voice was still gravelly, but there was a note of longing in it, and I had to look over my shoulder in surprise. His eyes were boring through me, hungrily, and for a split second, a very short second, I felt sorry for him. Then I turned straight again, and walked the last few steps towards the elevator.

Instead of heading to C-Deck, where my cabin was, I went all the way up to A-Deck—the bridge. I needed help. And information.

"Second medical officer on the bridge," I called, once the doors had slid open. "It's time for Lieutenant Howitz's checkup."

The Captain, August, and the two guards who stood with blasters on either side of the room, all looked around at me in surprise. "I didn't..." began August.

"But I did," I said crisply, adding a touch of professionalism to my voice. "He needs his blood pressure checked after that episode this afternoon."

The Captain seemed to catch on. "You heard the doctor, Lieutenant. To sickbay. Mr. Guilders can manage the course for awhile."

"It might be a couple of hours," I said as August stood and made his way towards me. "He'll need his rest."

"I understand," the Captain nodded.

I gestured for August to exit the bridge, and he did so, his pale face still showing definite signs of puzzlement. Nodding at the two guards, I followed him to the elevator.

"Andi, I..."

"I'll tell you what you need and what you don't need. Come on."

Once we were in the elevator, I breathed deeply and said, "I need your help. After I check you, we'll go to my quarters. You were sharing a cabin with your father, correct?"

"Yes, but he wanted me out once he used the machine."

"So you have not been assigned new quarters yet?"

"No. I still have two hours of duty."

"Then my cabin is the logical place. There's no camera in there, so we'll be safe."

He nodded, but looked worried. Before we had a chance to say more, the elevator reached B-Deck and we stepped out into the corridor.

We had to go into sickbay, and I had to scan him, for the benefit of the cameras. Then I spouted some doctor's talk, about the sympathetic nervous system and vasoconstriction of arterioles, before heading back out and down to C-Deck and my cabin.

I paused outside it and spoke loudly, trying to sound professional and not obviously loud. "You can rest in here until you get new quarters."

He caught on. "All right."

I unlocked the door and pushed him in, then followed and locked the door quickly.

"He has a camera outside your door?" he half-asked, half-stated.

I nodded. "They're in all the halls, and I have to assume he has one pointed at my door. Cameras don't work inside the cabins, because of the ISA privacy laws, but he wants to make sure those other guys can't get to me without him knowing it. As long as he watches my door, he should be safe."

"What did you want me for?" he asked quietly, his pale face struggling to stay calm.

Before explaining, I asked another question. "Why do you think he brought you here?"

He shrugged and looked away. "I don't know. I was doing just fine on the *Beagle*. He doesn't need my help. Probably he just thought it would be a good job for me, and wanted me around. I don't think he intended for things to go this way."

"He wants to kill me, you know."

"Andi!"

His face went paler, and his tone was utterly shocked.

"Sit down," I sighed. "You're going to give yourself another episode."

His hands trembling, he sat on my bed. "That's not true."

"It is. Maybe he doesn't want to kill me exactly, but I know he doesn't care that I'll die when he removes the radialloy."

"What?"

I pointed to my knee. "That's what he wants. It's the cure for a disease I have. If anyone takes it—the disease will kill me." I paused, letting him breathe deeply for a few minutes. Then, "What's he like?"

He fidgeted and traced the pattern on my blanket with one thin forefinger. "It's hard to say. He was always kind to me, he paid for whatever I wanted, let me do what I wanted. He can get a little angry when something goes really wrong, but he never took it out on me. He—he never talked about—either of you. It was like you'd never existed."

"You mean... me and—our mother?"

He nodded, not looking me in the eyes.

"What was *she* like?" I asked longingly.

For a moment longer he traced silently, then he stopped, reached into an inner pocket of his jacket, and pulled out a photograph. He handed it to me.

The woman who smiled up at me was less than ten years older than myself. Her hair was honey-golden, and her eyes, a soft brown, shone with a gentle, yet witty light.

I brushed a finger across her face while August began speaking.

"I was only five when she died. But I know she was pretty— and kind, and funny, and would always stop and play with me."

"Do you remember me?" I asked, handing the picture back

to him.

He made no move to take it. "Just a little."

I kept holding it out, but he shook his head. "You can keep it."

"August..."

"Please."

Biting my lip to keep the tears back, I put the picture in my own inner pocket, feeling a slight warmth settle in my heart.

"Why did you need me here?" he asked. "Was that all?"

"No." I walked over to my closet and opened a pair of doors in the bottom of it, revealing a set of shelves that were full of discarded machinery and other odds and ends. "We have to find some way to transmit a message to the *Alacrity I*. It's the closest vessel, and our only hope."

"Build a transmitter?" he asked, and I imagined his dark eyes growing wide. I heard him stand up, but I didn't turn around. I was busy sorting through different pieces, and I pulled a piece of fiber-optic cable from one shelf and deposited it in a pile on my left.

"Remember when the Doctor told you I liked inventing?" I kept on sorting, realizing for the first time that I'd probably inherited this propensity from Commander Howitz. "I'm going to put it to good use now."

August didn't say anything about that, but just sat down beside me and watched. "Where are you going to get enough power to transmit?"

I turned and looked at him seriously. "There are four generators on this ship."

"Two in engineering, one behind the bridge, and one in the galley," he nodded. "But you could never generate enough to transmit through subspace over two hundred parsecs, and the *Alacrity I* must be at least that far by now."

I continued my sorting, undisturbed. "I'll have to create an amplifier."

"But where are you going to get the materials for that? You

can't expect to formulate a transistor with all this."

"No."

"Then how?"

"I was thinking possibly I could construct a triode."

"A vacuum tube?" He looked thoughtfully at the pieces I had gathered around me. "Will that be strong enough? And are you sure you know how to do that?"

"All I know is, it's worth a try. Will you help me?"

Instead of answering, he sat down across from me, and asked, "Have you done anything like this before?"

"Not exactly. But I've been making little things for years. See this?" I held up a partial plastic tube, about a quarter of a meter long. "I was working on a portable chemical hand drier for the Doctor."

He took it and examined it for a moment. "Sensory release of silica gel?"

"Exactly." I pulled out a coil of wire. "He was always complaining about the blow driers." I swallowed hard, trying to keep the tears from coming.

Putting the drier down, he looked searchingly at me. "You really love him, don't you?"

"Yes."

"I wish I could help you."

Frustration boiled up inside me. He could help me, I knew he could, but he was too afraid.

As if reading my thoughts, he said hastily, "I don't like this—what Dad's doing. I'll help you with the transmitter." To prove it, he picked up a metal plate and handed it to me. "I just meant—I wish I could help you do something about your fath... about Doctor Lloyd."

"You can," I insisted, looking at him. "I'm going to find some way to get to the machine, and then you'll have to work it for me."

"I don't know how," he insisted. "Even if I did, there's no way to get to it."

"Nothing is completely foolproof. There has to be some way to override security on that door."

"But if he finds out what we're doing..."

"Sometimes you have to take risks, August!" I almost yelled. "If we don't try, there will be no chance at all." Grabbing up my pile of components, I stood up and hurried to my little table, where I dumped them.

There was silence for a moment as I made sure I had all the parts I needed. The wire—I must have dropped it—

His pale hand appeared in my peripheral vision, handing me the coil. I took it without looking up. "Thank you," I mumbled.

"I'm sorry," he said quietly, sitting at the table. "I'll try."

Timid or not, he was all I had right now. And his humble, "I'm sorry", which was something I would not have done, touched a chord in my heart. "Thanks. For now let's focus on building the transmitter."

"All right. What do you want me to do?"

I handed him a glass tube. "You're going to have to figure out how to create a vacuum."

CHAPTER XX

When we finished our work three hours later, I was thoroughly exhausted. After bidding me goodnight, he left to go get a new cabin, and I changed and dropped into bed, falling asleep almost instantly.

But it was not a restful sleep. My dreams were plagued with images of the Doctor lurching around the bridge, holding his head, with a look of intense pain on his face, and the Captain yelling frantic orders at officers who ignored his words, while a smiling Commander Howitz held a giant blaster that pointed at everyone at once, and August cowered in a corner. Guilders was never anywhere to be seen; he was invisible.

I bolted up when the Commander's blaster was fired in my dream, adrenaline rushing through my body. In a shocked state, I merely sat there for several minutes, staring at the bland wall of my quarters.

Then I let out a long breath. It had only been a dream.

Letting myself go limp, I dropped back down again and looked at the equally bland ceiling. I listened to the faint humming of the life support systems, then rolled over on my side and shut my eyes.

Finally I sat up, throwing the blankets off and swinging my legs over the side of the bed, letting them hit the floor hard. It was no use. I couldn't sleep.

Grabbing up my wristcom, I checked the time. 3:00. The day shift wouldn't begin for another three hours.

I strapped the com on and formed a decision. August had

told me for the reversal of eradication to work, the victim had to be in the same room as the device. So even once we got the machine away from Commander Howitz's quarters, we would have to get the Doctor as well. And right now, no one knew where he was.

I didn't allow my mind to suggest the possibility that we might not be able to get to the machine.

I dressed in the dark, feeling vaguely that the light would attract the attention of one of my adversaries, though the sensible part of me knew that was impossible. Then I unlocked my door and slipped out into the dim halls.

Although I knew it was futile, I tried his room first. It wasn't locked, and I peered in, my eyes still adjusted to the darkness.

Nothing. He wasn't there.

Fighting the urge to cry just at the sight of his empty room, I kept on down the hall resolutely. Someone, somewhere, had to know where he was.

For a moment I contemplated asking Commander Howitz to allow me to go see him. I quickly discarded the idea, however, when I remembered that he'd likely used the machine in the first place to keep me from consulting the Doctor. He would probably fear that if I saw him again now, I would be more unwilling than ever to come with him.

That was impossible, since I was already as unwilling as I could be to leave.

Shaking away these thoughts, I tried to think logically. Who might know where the Doctor was being held?

Well, what was keeping him from simply walking out of whatever room he was in? He must be guarded—at least, it was highly likely. As far as I knew, the majority of the mutineers, if not all of them, were from engineering.

And all but the first engineer's quarters were on D-Deck.

Deciding it was as good a theory as any, I slipped to the elevator and rode it down.

When the elevator doors opened again, the long row of

cabin doors made my spirits sink. I couldn't knock on every one of them. That would be absurd, and besides, someone was sure to realize what I was doing long before I was done.

Kerwin. The young man I'd treated the day of the mutiny. He was an engineering mate—surely he'd know something.

Kerwin—Merritt was his last name. I began walking down the hall, eyeing every name plate carefully. I tried to keep my boots from ticking on the hard floor as I stepped along, reading each name. No—not that one—that wasn't it—

There it was. *Ensign Kerwin Merritt.*

I raised my finger to press his door chime, then hesitated for an instant. It was so early—was it right to wake him?

This wasn't some ordinary situation. This was about life and death. He could get his sleep later.

Resolutely, I pressed the chime and waited. Silence for a moment, a moment in which he would have had plenty of time to get up and cross the room. I rang again.

This time it was only a few seconds before the door slid open and his youthful face appeared before me, blinking sleepily in the dim light. He looked so much younger when he was sleepy, I felt like I'd awakened a little boy, and a twinge of guilt pecked me. But I shook it off. This was no time for etiquette.

"Kerwin, it's me, Andi Lloyd," I said quietly.

"Yes?" he muttered, trying to open his eyes wider.

"I'm sorry to wake you, but it's important. Do you have any idea where they're keeping Doctor Lloyd? I need to find him, so I can help him."

He stared at me groggily, clearly trying to think. I fought back the urge to reach out, grab his shoulders and shake him. No matter that he was three inches taller than me, he still looked like a sleepy little boy.

"Doctor... Lloyd..." he muttered. "Doctor Lloyd... I think I heard something... just a minute..."

I bit my lip to keep myself from bursting with impatience. I didn't have a minute! We only had until noon to save the Doctor!

He opened his eyes a bit wider and the tiniest spark of realization appeared in them. "Doctor Lloyd, yes. I don't know the cabin number, but I know Ensign Shelhammer is guarding him. In his own room I think... there are two guards."

Shelhammer. I nodded as I impressed the name on my memory. "Thank you, Kerwin. I'm sorry I woke you."

"Any time," he murmured, retreating into the room and letting the door close again.

I crept down the hall, scanning the name plates for a "Shelhammer." It was at the far end of the hall—"Ensign Darren Shelhammer." I didn't know him—he was probably a part of the night crew.

Suppressing the knotty feeling in the pit of my stomach, I pressed the door chime and waited.

This time I didn't have to push it twice. Before I expected it, the door shot open and a stern, stalwart, broad-shouldered man appeared before me, blaster in hand.

Recovering from the silence the shock had forced on me, I spoke falteringly. "I'm—I'm Andi Lloyd. I just—is the Doctor awake?"

He furrowed his brows. "Why?"

"I just—want to see him." I looked pleadingly into the man's eyes. Surely he would see how desperate I was. "I just want to see how he's doing, only for a moment."

He looked doubtfully at me, the inflexibility of his expression not abating. We stood like this for a moment, then I heard another voice. "What is it, Darren?"

Another crewman, shorter and slighter, pushed past the first one. He saw me then, and looked sorry. "Miss Lloyd."

I nodded. I recognized him, though I didn't know his name. He'd been in sickbay the week before, and I'd helped the Doctor set his broken finger.

"You just wanted to visit your father?"

"I wanted to see the Doctor, yes."

He looked up at the taller guard. "She can come in for a

moment." This was said in a quiet but authoritative tone.

Darren looked unsure about this. "But the Commander said..."

Without acknowledging that his partner had spoken, the shorter guard nodded at me. "Only a moment."

Looking my thanks, I moved past the men into the room, trying not to tremble with fear of what I might find there.

Even after the dim corridors, the room was dark. I could just barely make out a thin form seated in a low chair in one corner. The Doctor.

His head was bowed stiffly over his hands, which were laying listlessly across his bony knees.

As my eyes became more accustomed to the gloom, I saw that his face was dazed and moist, and water covered the front of his half-open shirt and had dripped down onto his pant legs. He stared at his hands, and didn't look up as I approached. Tears ran down my cheeks unchecked as I noted the gauntness of his cheekbones and the increased lines on his forehead. I hardly recognized him.

Kneeling in front of him, I took his damp hands in mine. His fingers were wrinkled from excessive immersion in water, and his skin was cold and clammy. Looking up into his eyes, I pleaded, "Doctor, do you know me?"

There was a moment of silence, then he looked into my face. "Remind me again of your name?"

"Andi. It's me, Andi."

There was a momentary pause, then he spoke slowly, his voice quiet and tense. "I knew someone by that name. She was my daughter."

"That's me. I am your daughter, Doctor."

He looked me in the eyes, and hazy surprise registered. "Lavinia? What are you doing here? Where is Sara?"

I squeezed his hands gently. "Sara's gone. It's me, Andi."

He looked down at my hands, and his trembled. Then he looked closely at me again. There was a moment of gripping silence as he studied my face, and then a flash of recognition lit up his eyes. He grasped my hands tighter. "Andi!"

I smiled through my tears. "Doctor, we know what's wrong with you."

"What's wrong with me?"

"Yes. We're going to help you. We're going to help you remember everything again."

He sighed. "I don't understand what you're saying."

"You don't have to. Don't worry. Just try to hang on until I come back. Try to remember."

"Remember what?"

I leaned close to him. "Do you remember the time Crash took us out for our first space flight? You got sick."

He looked confused again. "Crash?"

"Eagle Crash, your nephew. Do you remember him? Do you remember when your parents died and you had to raise Sara by yourself? Do you remember when she married Miles Crash and left you alone? Do you remember when she died, and Crash came to live with us? Don't you remember, Doctor?"

His fingers gripped tighter, and his face twisted as he tried desperately to recall the things I said. "Crash... Sara... Sara was my sister. You were her best friend. She had blonde hair and blue eyes."

I had never met the beautiful Sara Crash, but I had seen pictures of her. I nodded.

"She left me alone. My parents left me. Journey left me."

My tears started up again. He'd rarely talked to me about his parents, and I didn't know who Journey was. But it was clear that he was remembering.

"Then I found the child. She needed me. I took her because I had to, but I kept her because I loved her. She did not leave me."

My heart threatened to break. "Doctor..." my trembling voice began, but a hand was laid firmly on my shoulder, and the guard named Darren spoke.

"You should go now."

Before standing up, I gave his hands one last squeeze and whispered, "I trust you, Doctor. I'll be back—we'll save you. Wait for me—keep remembering."

The lost look had come back to his face, but he nodded before looking back down at his wet hands. "I must wash my hands," he said softly. "I must wash them."

Guided through the dark by the tall lieutenant, I stumbled out of the room and just barely took the time to grasp the other guard's hand warmly for a moment before stepping out into the comparative brightness of the corridor. The door slid shut behind me.

It took me several moments to recover sufficiently to even walk down the hall. I rubbed the rough sleeve of my uniform across my eyes, trying to wipe away the tears.

Now I knew where he was. I had to think. We still had get to the machine—and then get him out. Then we had to work the machine—but we also had to get help. We couldn't get the ship back on our own. The Commander and the two scientists were too smart for that.

I had to outsmart them. Glancing at my wristcom, I saw that it was already past four. Could it really have been over an hour since I woke up?

I couldn't wait any longer to contact Crash. If I did, he wouldn't be able to make it in time to help us.

CHAPTER XXI

Slipping down the empty corridors, I tried to relax, to keep my heart beating at a normal rate as it threatened to accelerate. Taking a deep breath, I stepped into the elevator and directed it to take me to C-Deck. From there I hurried to my quarters and picked up the transmitter we'd built the night before. It was too large to hide beneath my jacket—but there was a brown shoulder bag hanging from a hook next to my closet. I used it sometimes to carry medical supplies.

Grabbing it, I thrust the transmitter in. It kept the bag from closing all the way, but the flap went far enough to hide it and not attract attention. That would have to do.

I hurried to the mess hall, hoping that I could finish before it opened. Because of my frequent service there, I had complete access to it, so I should have no problem getting to the generator. What I would have a problem with, I realized, was actually running the generator. There was no way I could generate the power needed. I didn't think August could either—and running my eyes mentally over Kerwin's slight, boyish figure, I didn't think he could do it.

There was nothing to do but try it. I could think of something later if that didn't work.

The mess hall was empty and almost completely dark when I entered. I didn't dare activate the lights, for fear of attracting attention, so I wove my way carefully through the mass of tables and chairs.

"Oomph!" I struggled to repress a cry as the back of a chair unexpectedly plunged into the pit of my stomach. I rubbed it, squinting, and gave the seat a wide berth.

I knew the way well enough that I was able to make it to the bar without any more mishaps, and I slipped behind the bar, keeping one hand on the transmitter to protect it.

I felt over the wall beside the galley door until my fingers found the keypad, then I visualized where the numbers were in my mind and entered the access code. After letting off a beep that made me cringe by its contrast to the silence, it blinked green and the door slid open.

It was dark in there, too, though not as black as the mess hall. Green and blue lights from the temperature regulators and ovens gave the room a spooky and unnerving aspect, but I walked in bravely, letting the door slide shut behind me.

With the help of the lights, it was easy to find my way across the room to the pantry door. My footsteps echoed off the metal floor, but I kept reassuring myself that there was no one near enough to hear them. When I reached the pantry, I entered the access code with confidence. It was a good thing I had such a good head for numbers.

I took one step into the pitch black pantry, and then a hand gripped my shoulder. With a shriek, I fought against it, pulling away into the shelves ahead of me.

"Andi?" A voice hissed at my ear. "Is that you?"

I stopped fighting as I recognized the voice. It was Edwardo, the young galley assistant.

Turning, I looked where I thought his eyes must be. "Yes, it's me." I kept my voice in a whisper, as he had. "What are you doing here?"

"I'm supposed to open snack bar in a few minutes, for the night crew," he said, quietly, but not in a whisper. Letting go of my shoulder, he reached back and turned on a light. I blinked in the unexpected brightness and squinted up at his strong, dark face. "What are you doing here?"

I hesitated. Could I trust him? I had met him occasionally

while helping out, and he'd always been nice to me. But then, so had Mr. Jarvis, and he was helping the mutineers.

"I'm on the Captain's side," he reassured, as if answering my unspoken question.

Still, I hesitated. Then, eyeing his muscular arms and strong, broad-shouldered form, I decided to take a chance. He could help me.

I pulled the transmitter from the bag and held it up. "I need to contact my cousin, Eagle Crash."

His brown eyes widened. "So... you need to use the generator?"

I nodded. "Can you get it going?"

For an instant he just looked at me, and I felt fear rise in my stomach. Would he betray me?

Finally he started towards the back of the room, where the generator chamber was. "We need to hurry."

I ran after him, and watched as he opened the door and slipped in. I followed, and when he turned on the light I beheld the long, cylindrical generator in the middle of the tiny, oddly shaped chamber, it's giant crank sticking out towards us and multiple wires connecting it to circuit boards covering the walls.

Edwardo stepped forward and surveyed the wires that emerged from the machine, then the gadget in my hand.

"How many connections can it take?" he asked.

"Five."

He blew out slowly, then approached one of the panels. "I think the connections to the ovens make the most efficient use of power."

I nodded, and nervously pulled out the long antenna as he began carefully unplugging different connections. "I'm not an electrical engineer or anything," he cautioned, "but I'll see what I can do."

After a moment he held out his hand for the transmitter, and I handed it to him, not without trepidation. It was delicate, and the smallest mistake could render it useless.

But he handled it gently, and lifted it above his head, rather than turning it upside-down, to plug the cables into the bottom. After several tensely quiet moments, he handed it back to me. "Should I go ahead and start the generator?"

I nodded, and began turning the rather crude dial to modulate the frequency. I hoped I'd been able to get it precise enough to get to the *Alacrity*'s frequency, which I knew by heart—189.4 gigahertz.

Edwardo had begun turning the crank, and it squeaked at first, making me cringe. The generator began to whine, a low rumbling whine first, slowly getting higher and faster as he turned.

"Got it yet?" I murmured.

He looked at the gauge, sweat already beginning to drip from his forehead. "Not yet," he grunted.

The steady hum grew as he cranked. I stood there, waiting.

A moment later, he announced, "Now."

I flipped on the transmitter, looking at the tiny indicator. It said we were at 188.9. I turned it slightly, which brought it to 190.8.

Biting my lip, I laid my finger on the dial and moved it as little as I could. It now read 189.0.

I pressed my finger carefully on the dial, attempting to turn clockwise less than a millimeter. It was raised to 189.5.

Biting harder, I jiggled the transmitter. The indicator slipped to 189.4.

I locked the dial, then pressed the transmission button and slipped my headset on to wait for connection to be established.

"Hurry," he grunted, still cranking vigorously.

A wave of static came over my headphones, and I began to speak. "*Alacrity I*, this is Andi Lloyd. Crash, do you read?"

For a second, the only sound that met my ears was sporadic buzzing. But then, a fuzzy voice crackled through.

"Andi, I can barely hear you. This is Prescott Whales."

"Mr. Whales, our ship has been taken over by Commander Howitz. We are being forced to take him to sector four-thousand."

"We've been... to contact... couldn't find..."

"Mr. Whales, please help us!"

"Come... sector..."

Static obscured most of his words. Edwardo cranked with all his might, but I was losing the connection.

"Sector four-thousand, Mr. Whales. Commander Howitz is forcing us to travel to sector four-thousand." I said each word carefully and clearly, hoping desperately that he would be able to understand.

"We'll try..."

Light appeared under the door, and I dropped the transmitter. Edwardo let go of the crank and jumped out of the way to keep from being hit by its inertial spinning. Grabbing the transmitter, he disconnected it from the cables and shoved it into my arms. As we heard footsteps outside the door, he pushed me to the back of the room and opened a small cabinet door in the darkest corner. "Get in."

Without stopping to think, I crawled in desperately and he slammed the door shut behind me.

I held my breath, listening anxiously. For a second, I only heard Edwardo's footsteps as he walked back to the center of the room, then the whir of the generator stopped.

For a fraction of a second there was nothing, then the sound of the door opening broke the silence.

"What are you doing here?" asked an insisting voice. "Why isn't snack bar open yet?"

"The ovens weren't working, sir." Edwardo's voice was confident. "I came to check the connections, and see if running the generator would help."

There was more silence, and then a few more footsteps.

"Have you seen Andi Lloyd anywhere?"

"Yes sir, I saw her this morning."

My heart rose in my throat, and a scream rose with it. I had to force myself not to clap my hand to my mouth.

"She was just coming out of her room, I think she was going

to sickbay."

My heart settled again.

Another silence. I breathed gently, trying not to make a sound.

"Open the snack bar immediately."

"Yes sir."

There was one more brief silence, then the footsteps retreated, and the door slid closed. I waited for a moment, not sure whether it was safe to come out or not. But before much time had elapsed, the cabinet door opened, letting the dim light of the chamber in. Edwardo's dark, worried face met mine. "Come on," he whispered, "he's gone."

I took his offered hand and he helped me climb out. "Thank you," I gasped, trying to get my bearings.

Nodding, he led me through the pantry, flipping on the light as he entered. "You'd better leave right away."

"Thank you," I said again as we stepped out into the galley.

"Try not to attract too much attention," he whispered.

In a sudden motion, I pulled the transmitter out of my bag and handed it to Edwardo, who looked blankly at it. "Crush it and throw it in the recyclator," I insisted. "I wouldn't want them to search me and find it."

Nodding, he took it and carried it over to the other side of the room. I took a deep breath, then rushed out. I'd have to find someone to help me get the Doctor out of his detention, and then somehow get hold of the deadly machine. How? How could we do those things?

A solitary man sat at the counter as I stepped into the snack bar, and for an instant my heart jumped in fear. Was it the man who had come looking for me? He would know Edwardo had lied!

Then I breathed a sigh of relief. It was Guilders.

"You're—you're up so early!" I stammered.

"It is past five," he said stoically, leaning his folded hands on the counter. "I go on duty in a little over an hour. How are you doing?"

I shook my head. "May I sit here?" I patted the stool next to him.

"Certainly."

I sat down. "Have you become invisible yet?"

"I think so. My wristcom is still being allowed to transmit."

There was a silence as I swallowed and licked my lips. Then, "I need your help."

He looked at me expectantly. "Oh?"

"Yes." Looking down, I twisted a corner of my jacket. "We have to free the Doctor, and then get the machine out of Commander Howitz's quarters."

"That memory eradicator that Lieutenant Howitz told us about?"

"Yes. I'm going to convince August to work it. But first I have to get the Doctor out and get the machine." I lowered my voice. "I already contacted the *Alacrity I.*"

He was silent for a moment, then he shifted on the stool. "Do you know where Gerard is?"

"Yes," I said eagerly, looking up to meet his calm eyes. "I saw him early this morning. He's in Ensign Shelhammer's quarters, guarded by two men. He's—" I choked a little. "He's so broken down. He's losing everything."

Again, he didn't speak for a moment. But he furrowed his bushy gray eyebrows far more than usual, so that I could see he was deep in thought.

"Do you know how to work the security systems?" he asked at last.

I shook my head.

Another moment of thinking, then he flattened his hands on the counter and looked at me. "Ralston would know, and I'd trust him. If you and he can manage to get to the central security chamber, then I have an idea. But once you did that you'd have to get Gerard out quickly before Commander Howitz realized what had happened. How many hours left?"

"Just about five." I bit my lip, my heart beginning to speed up again.

He nodded. "All right. Are you willing to take risks?"

I didn't hesitate for a moment. "Yes."

"All right. I'll send Ralston here, and then here's what you'll have to do..."

CHAPTER XXII

Mr. Ralston and I crept through the dark storage chamber above B-Deck, not daring to speak. Crates and dormant machinery lay on all sides of the vast space, neatly separated, numbered and stacked. At the far end of the room were the security panels, where a lone technician worked in silence.

Not letting our boots make a sound against the hard floor, we slipped closer and closer, until we were right behind the crewman. Then in a sudden motion, Mr. Ralston reached out and gripped the man around the neck with one arm, using his other hand to cover the unfortunate worker's mouth. With equal speed, I pulled a full hypo from my bag and injected the man with an intravenous sedative.

For another moment Mr. Ralston continued gripping him, then he went limp, and the data controller laid him carefully down.

"Isn't that against the Hippocratic oath?" he asked, his thin lips giving a slight smile as he turned to the panel.

I shrugged as I put the hypo back in the bag. "I've never taken it."

"How long will he be out?"

"Maybe half an hour."

"That should be plenty of time," Ralston observed, and began to scan through the security subsystems. I watched, even though I was unable to follow what he was doing.

He found the cabin security section and murmured, "What's the cabin number?"

I blushed as I realized I'd forgotten to find out. "I'm—I'm

not sure. I think about... it's halfway down the hall on C-Deck, I think if you're coming from the lounge, it's on your right somewhere."

Nodding, he navigated through the system then stood up straight and spoke quietly. "Got it. To be unlocked only with clearance from the man himself." He turned to look at me, his eyes looking wide in his thin face. "If this doesn't work?"

I shrugged, trying to hide my trembling. "We'll get out of here before he realizes what happened. He won't know we were the ones who tried it." I wasn't convincing myself, and I doubted I was convincing him either.

Clenching my teeth, I took the last step to the console. Ralston pressed a button, lighting up a small green panel. "Ready for clearance scan," a computerized voice said, making me cringe. I hesitated for a moment, then laid my hand on the little panel.

I watched as a green bar of light moved over the panel, slowly moving from my wrist to the tips of my fingers. It gave off just enough heat for me to feel it as it passed, and I forced myself to stop trembling.

The light finished scanning and seemed to hesitate. I stiffened. If this didn't work, an alarm would be set off throughout the ship, and despite my assurances to Ralston, I wasn't sure we'd be able to escape detection.

Then, a clear, ringing beep sounded. "DNA—Howitz, Erasmus, Commander. Security cleared." Then there was a clicking sound, and the panel turned off.

I pulled my hand away, letting my breath come quickly. It had worked! Guilders hadn't been positive that it would interpret my DNA as his, but it had. Now we could just walk into his room.

After stepping backwards for a few steps, I turned to face Mr. Ralston. "Tell Guilders it worked."

He nodded and started back towards the elevator. I let him use it first, as we were going opposite directions—he up to the bridge to tell Guilders to send August to sickbay, I down to sickbay to wait for my brother.

My mind turned back to the Doctor as I waited for the elevator to come back down. We had just four hours to save him! My stomach began churning as I waited—and waited—I began picking at my jacket button and scraping my boots along the floor. We had to save him.

What if I have another plan? A voice whispered. I slammed the door on the voice, feeling my heart scream. *Don't say that, God! You wouldn't do that, I know you wouldn't.*

At last the smooth doors in front of me slid open, and I jumped in, not even waiting for them to finish sliding. "B-Deck!" I snapped, feeling somehow as though the elevator were to blame for my disturbing thoughts.

Who knew how long it would take Guilders to get August down to sickbay? He'd said it could be awhile. By that time, the security guard might wake up, and warn Commander Howitz. Then the Commander would lock his quarters again, and we wouldn't have another chance.

We should have gotten August down first. I knew why Guilders had decided not to do that—he worried that if Commander Howitz did realize what we'd done, it would be worse for August if he were found missing from his post. We had to make sure it would work first.

Maybe I could go in and find the machine without August.

I didn't know what it looked like—but how hard could it be to find it? It was a machine—surely I could figure it out. It would probably have some kind of identifying mark on it.

No. I shouldn't. Guilders knew we were in a hurry, he'd get August down right away. He'd find some way to do it, I knew he would. I would just have to trust him.

The elevator stopped on B-Deck, and the doors opened. I lifted one foot to step out, to walk down the hall to sickbay, to wait for August's help.

Then I put my foot down again, stood up straight, and said, "C-Deck."

The doors closed again, and I was moved down. I couldn't

do it. I had to get down there now and get that machine, before it was too late.

I *wouldn't* let the Doctor go crazy—or die.

When it stopped, I leapt out into the corridor, afraid that if I hesitated I'd change my mind.

It was easy to find his cabin, and when I had, I stopped in front of it and took a deep breath. Then I jammed my thumb recklessly on the open button to the right of the door.

For a crazed half-second, nothing happened. Then the door slid open welcomingly, without letting off so much as a squeak.

It had worked! Everything would be all right!

Jubilant, I slipped into the room and looked around. It was a duplicate of every other officer's cabin, except for a row of large, somewhat frightening devices on a metal chest on the far side of the room.

I walked towards them, not allowing myself to give in to the urge to tip-toe. I had to figure out which one was the right one, and figure it out quickly.

There were five items on the chest, neatly lined up in a row. All five were of different shapes and sizes, though they were all varying shades of gray and black. My heart sank a little when I saw that none of them bore any characters of any kind—neither letters nor numbers indicated the type of device.

Still. I was good at inventions and mechanics, I could figure it out. August had mentioned x-rays—so which one of these could produce x-rays? It would have to be capable of extreme precision to lock onto specific sections of the brain, so I instantly ruled out the simple apparatus on the far left. The controls on the center machine didn't look complex enough either...

"You do me credit, my dear."

My blood froze as my heart stopped beating. The voice was a low, gravelly one that I knew well.

I hadn't heard the door open, but the sound of boots stalking towards me was all too clear. I swallowed, feeling somehow that if I just kept still and didn't turn around, I wouldn't have to deal with the situation, and everything would be all right.

"I'd hardly hoped that even with my genes you could have become so inventive," he continued. "Unfortunately, you picked the wrong moment to enter. I happened to have this hall's security camera on the screen."

Dull pain engulfed my heart. *The wrong moment.* Yes, it had been the wrong moment. A few minutes later, and we would have succeeded.

Andi, you fool!

"I had hoped that you would trust me," he went on, and his strong hands gripped both my arms in a hold that made me wince. "But I'm going to have that metal one way or another."

With a forcefulness that didn't match his calm, calculated words, he pulled me back. I grunted and struggled to pull away, knowing all the while that it was useless.

My efforts only made him clutch me tighter, and I felt my lower arms begin to tingle with constricted blood flow. I couldn't call for help—I couldn't fight him. Could I reason with him?

"Father," I begged. "Please! I just wanted the Doctor back..."

Without even acknowledging that I'd spoken, he turned and began pushing me towards a metal closet on the other side of the room. Taking one hand off of me, he pushed a button to open the door. I took the opportunity to pull against him and try to wrench his hold off with my free hand, but once again it did me no good. I twisted around and tried blindly to kick him in the shin, but he gripped my other arm again and held me at arm's length, facing him.

I stopped struggling and stared into his eyes, which were a warring combination of hatred, hunger, despair and triumph. The triumph I understood, but the rest left me confused.

After ten seconds of silence, he spoke. "Genevieve Lavinia Sandison. You were named after *her*. Her! You bear her name, her face—her determined..." he choked, and the other emotions were swallowed up by loathing.

Understanding flashed upon me. He'd told me that Langham's Disease could only be contracted by babies—and by pregnant women.

He heaved me into the closet, and my head hit the hard, metal back. I was dazed, but before he closed the door I addressed him once again. "She had the disease, didn't she?"

He stopped his hand midway to the button and stared at me, his small pupils constricting more than ever.

I sat up straight and looked him straight in the eyes.

"My mother," I went on. "She had Langham's Disease, didn't she?"

The hate stared out of his eyes, but I was unabashed.

"You didn't get enough of the cure before the mine was destroyed," I said slowly, figuring it out as I went along. "You only got enough for me."

"We didn't know!" he almost screamed, clapping his palms on both sides of the door and leaning inward.

I didn't shrink back. "So you wanted to take my radialloy and give it to her. You wanted to sacrifice my life for hers."

"I loved her!" he cried. "You can't even begin to understand how much I loved her! I wanted to save her!"

"By killing me?" I cried.

"It wasn't killing you! You would have died in the first place if it weren't for me! You *killed* her!"

My eyes tingled with unshed tears, but I kept on, my voice beginning to waver. "Did you tell her your plan? Or did she find it out?"

"Do you really think I would have *told* her?"

"So she took me away. She took me—where I would be safe." Fierce pain grabbed my heart as I thought of the Doctor.

"If it weren't for you, if it weren't for *him*, she would still be alive!" A paroxysm of fury contorted his face, and the last vestige of pretense fell away. "You deserve to die!" He pounded his fist on the button and the metallic door slammed shut, leaving me locked in darkness.

I didn't hear his footsteps as he left the room, but I felt no doubt that he had. My bravado drained out of me, and I sank to the floor, resting my back against the cold, metal wall of the closet.

Even if August and Guilders realized what I had done, my father would have locked the door, and he'd be watching the systems now. The trick wouldn't work twice. And there were just over three hours left to save the Doctor.

Why, why didn't I just stick with the plan? Oh why couldn't I have just done what Guilders and my conscience said to do?

The same reason I hadn't listened when the Doctor told me not to listen to Erasmus.

I trusted myself before all others.

I was so desperate to keep things the way I wanted them, that I couldn't let the future rest in anyone's hands but my own.

As it had turned out, my hands were anything but competent.

My wristcom let off a tiny, faint square of green light, and I could read the black numbers flicking from digit to digit on it as the seconds went by. A minute. Two minutes. Five minutes. Thirty. I heard nothing, felt nothing but the cold metal through my jacket and the course fibers of the Commander's uniform against my cheek.

Fifty minutes. There were only two and a half hours left until twelve.

Something snapped inside me, and I dropped my head to my knees, hugging them to my chest. I sobbed, releasing pent-up tears that did nothing to relieve the horrible, consuming ache in my heart.

After endless long minutes of sobbing and numbing, I felt myself drifting, moving away from reality. I wasn't worried about suffocation in the closet, for a thin crack under the door provided air.

So I let myself drift. There was nothing I could do. Nothing. I couldn't even try any longer. All I could do was to sit, and condemn myself.

One moment I was slipping out of consciousness, the next I was jolted awake by a sudden feeling that I was falling. Feeling momentarily disoriented, I reached up to brush something from my cheek and felt a uniform pant leg.

Then my head cleared, and I sat up straight.

A beep startled me, causing me to hit my head on the back of the closet. Then the door slid open, and I blinked, dazed in the sudden light.

Two men stood there, but at first I could only make out blurry forms. I saw that one was short and one was tall and bulky, which led me to guess that it was Peat and Sigmet. When my vision sharpened, my guess was confirmed.

"Hurry," said Sigmet, beckoning with one rounded hand. Peat held a small electronic device, pointing at the closet lock. He lowered it as I stood up. "We have to get out before he finds us."

I didn't see how I could be any worse off with them than with him, so I stepped out of the closet.

A thought made my stomach tie itself in knots. "Did they save the Doctor?" I asked.

Peat slipped the device in his pocket and gripped my arm in one continuous motion, then began pulling me along.

My heart hurting until I couldn't bear it, I managed to look at my wristcom as he dragged me out.

It was three minutes past twelve.

"Answer my question, or I'll scream," I cried as we rushed out into the bright, white corridor.

"Don't be a fool," Peat insisted.

But Sigmet said, "No. He's still in captivity."

My world ended.

It was too late.

CHAPTER XXIII

They continued to drag me down the hall, and for several minutes I was too devastated to notice or care where they were taking me. We rode the elevator up, and then they hurried me out and into the B-Deck hall.

"*...twenty hours. That's until he goes insane. After that, if he's not taken care of in another twenty-four—he'll die.*"

I jerked up as I remembered August's words. We still had time to save him.

Competing emotions tore at me—my heart sank like lead as I thought of him never being sane again, and yet at the thought that his life might be saved, adrenaline surged through my veins.

Where were they taking me? What were they going to do with me? Would they hide me somewhere else, so Commander Howitz couldn't get to me again?

As we got closer and closer to the end of the hall, the side of the ship, I understood. They were taking me to their speeder.

But—how could they use it without the Commander's clearance...

Unless they knew how I'd gotten in his room. The same method would probably work on the speeder.

Instinctively, I jerked my hands behind my back. They couldn't know. How could they? Guilders and Ralston were the only other people who knew what had happened, and neither of them would tell.

But something told me that the men who could stop security cameras and get through locked doors with a little metal device could figure out anything they wanted.

My idea was confirmed as the large airlock doors at the end of the hall came into view.

I wasn't going to go with them. I had to save the Doctor. Somehow.

Letting my heart beat twice, I gave my arm a wrench, trying to pry it from Peat's grasp. If he was surprised, he didn't show a sign of it. His hold didn't loosen, and he continued jogging towards the airlock.

"No!" I screamed. I tried to plant my feet on the floor, but they slid easily. As we passed the last quarters door, I tried to grab on to it, but we were too far away.

He pulled me through the huge doorway, and I grabbed onto the edge of it with my free hand, clamping my fingers as tightly as I could manage. I would *not* go.

He kept tugging on me for a moment, and a wave of pain shot over my shoulder. My knuckles cracked painfully, and my fingers slid slowly over the edge, but I didn't give up.

"Help!" I screamed. "Hel..."

Sigmet clapped a hand over my mouth and pulled my hand forcibly from the door. The speeder was moored inside, I saw the access opening into a small craft.

Together, they dragged me towards the access panel. I struggled, tried to scream, but the short man's hand effectively blocked any sound.

Peat used his free hand to activate the panel.

"Ready for clearance scan," came the computerized voice.

I pulled harder than ever. Peat pulled my hand close to the panel, but adrenaline seemed to give me superhuman strength, and I pulled back, adhering my boots to the smooth metal floor somehow.

Sigmet let go of my arm and gave me a push in the back. I stumbled forward, and felt my hand pressed to the warm surface of the scanner. But he had also let go of my mouth, and I screamed again.

I heard a sound, like something bouncing twice on metal, and then arms encircled Peat's neck from the back and he was yanked away.

The big man let go of my hand to try to disengage the newcomer's arms, and I jumped away from the panel. In a second, Sigmet had grabbed both of my wrists and had started forcing me towards the scanner again, but I kicked him in the shin and he grunted and let go long enough for me to duck down out of reach of his grasping arms and dash for the back of the room.

Then I looked back towards the struggle.

August!

August, his face paler than ever, fought both men, but he was losing the battle. Even if he were strong and completely healthy, he would have been no match for the two men, or even Peat alone. I clapped my hands over my mouth as Sigmet grabbed his left arm and twisted it behind him, causing August to let out a scream.

"Sometimes you have to take risks, August..."

The scream woke me up. He wasn't fighting them to win. He was fighting them to give me a chance to get away.

I knew what I'd have to do.

Without waiting another second, I tore my gaze away from the struggle and ran, ran out of the airlock and down the corridor. I didn't look or listen to see if they'd noticed that I'd left, I just ran. Ran, ran, ran, finally reaching the elevator.

It opened, ready for me, and I jumped in. For a split second I hesitated, then followed my instincts and yelled, "A-Deck!"

The elevator seemed to rush faster than usual, and yet at the same time it seemed to take longer. I gripped the rail that ran along the wall, feeling the pain still throbbing in my knuckles.

Finally the elevator came to a crisp stop, and I was out almost before the door opened. From there it was only a few leaps to the bridge doors, which slid open unasked when I reached them.

I took in the room at a single glance. There he was, standing beside the Captain's chair, face furrowed in stony frustration.

"Commander Howitz!" I yelled. "They have August!"

Silence reigned. He turned slowly to look at me, anger shooting from his face. "How did you..."

"Never mind that!" I cried, jumping forward. "Peat and Sigmet! They have August in the airlock. They're hurting..."

Before I could say another word, he was out of the command pit and at the door. "Martin, keep an eye on things!" he called. "You, come with me."

He looked at me as he said "you," and I hastened to follow. I had only a second in which to decide whether or not to obey, and it was enough. I had to look after August if he was hurt, and if I didn't come, I felt sure that the Commander would only force me.

Not a word was said as we rode the elevator back down to C-Deck and rushed through the halls. He didn't question me, he only ran. I panted as I tried to keep up with him, using two steps to his one.

"DNA—Howitz, Erasmus, Commander. Security cleared," the computer voice rang out as we approached the airlock.

The Commander bounded the last few meters to the entrance, and I heard shouts of surprise. Breathing hard, I reached the opening at last and looked in.

The Commander thumped a large fist on Peat's head, then twisted his arm behind his back and yanked his blaster from its holster at his belt. Tossing the blaster into the corner, he released the man and drew his own weapon in a single, fluid movement, then stepped back and surveyed the two men. Sigmet hadn't had time to draw his own, and made no move to draw it now.

August lay senseless on the floor, blood steadily trickling from a gash in his forehead. I cried out and started to dash to his side, but the Commander's voice stopped me.

"Just a moment, Genevieve. Take Mr. Sigmet's blaster from his belt."

I tried to swallow, but a nervous lump prevented it. I walked the two steps to the odd little man's side and pulled his blaster from his belt, never meeting his eyes. Then I stepped back.

"Point it at them," he ordered.

I did so, settling my finger tremblingly on the trigger.

"Now." He said it calmly, his gravelly voice drawing the syllable out uncomfortably. "Over to that corner, away from the entrance."

Peat's eyes were angry, but Sigmet's high ones didn't change. They shuffled a few meters to their left.

"Keep them covered, Andi." Lowering his weapon, he walked to the panel and began to work it.

Peat's eyes dared me to fire if he moved, and I stared back with all the sternness I could muster.

"I believe you've broken our deal, gentlemen," the Commander said coolly, continuing his work for a moment. Then the computer announced, "Mooring locked." The Commander turned around.

"You're the one who broke it!" Peat exploded. "Locking the girl away? That wasn't part of..."

"She was interfering. What made you think that I wouldn't follow through with our agreement?"

They seemed to have no answer to this. Sigmet asked coldly, "Just what is your plan now, Sandison?"

As a reply, the Commander pushed a button on his wristcom and spoke into it. "Two armed officers to airlock one at once."

"Yes sir," a voice answered.

"Arresting us?" asked Sigmet coldly.

"Yes. I can no longer trust you."

"Don't play games with us," Sigmet scoffed. "You never trusted us."

"That doesn't really matter now, does it? On second thought, you cause more trouble than I care for. Perhaps I should just dispense with you..."

"Commander!" I cried.

"...unless you'd like to show your worth by telling me the

clearance code for the piloting of your ship."

So my guess earlier had been right. Neither could take me before because neither could leave without clearance from the other. If he could get the code from them, there'd be nothing stopping him from just taking me and leaving right now. I bit my lip.

Peat looked haughty. "Nice try, Sandison."

Even as he spoke, I understood. He wouldn't kill them. If he did, he'd never be able to use the speeder.

Two uniformed crewmen appeared with drawn blasters in the doorway. Commander Howitz looked at them and cocked his head towards his co-conspirators. "Take them to the brig."

They didn't argue. They were both too smart for that. The crewmen shifted around behind them and pointed their blasters at their backs at point blank range. "You heard the Commander."

Not even waiting for them to make it out the door, the Commander turned to me, resheathing his blaster. "How is he?"

He... August. I dropped the blaster I was holding and knelt by his side. The blood had already slowed, but he was still pale and his breathing was shallow. I almost sighed.

"He's in the early stages of shock," I announced, feeling his wrist. "We'd better get him to sickbay."

Without a word, he hoisted August up in his powerful, muscular arms, and started towards sickbay.

CHAPTER XXIV

I followed, not thinking of escape for the moment. My brother needed me. The walls seemed to glide smoothly past, and the elevator door to slide towards us, and I barely felt my boots touch the floor as I hurried after him.

The elevator carried us to B-Deck, and the Commander, bearing his still unconscious son, turned fluidly to the right as he exited. I followed, not as fluidly, almost hopping to keep up with his huge strides.

At last we reached sickbay, and he burst through the door and lay August down on one of the cots with surprising gentleness. Then he turned to me and said, his gravelly voice as collected as ever, "Take care of him."

He said it as though committing a charge to me, and I hoped that he would leave the room, but instead he simply positioned himself at the end of the bed and stood there, arms folded over his chest, watching.

I cleared my throat, finding myself suddenly nervous. I'd never been nervous when the Doctor watched me. But with a struggle, I switched my brain to professional mode and examined the small gash on his forehead.

My hands trembled as I reached for the regen kit in the medical cabinet. *Be all right, August.* If I had gone to sickbay to meet him like I was supposed to—

We could be winning right now. August could be fine, we could all be safe, the Doctor—he could be all right.

Stop thinking. Just work.

With a great effort of will, I blotted out my fears and set to work on healing August's cut and getting his blood pressure back up. Commander Howitz only watched, silently, from the corner, his arms crossed over his chest. I tried to forget he was there, but he was still fuzzily impressed on some corner of my brain as I worked, like a little gray cloud in a clear, cold sky.

Other than the subtle consciousness of his presence, I knew nothing except the necessity of healing. The steady slowing of my brother's pulse and breath rate, the slow regeneration of skin as the drug worked on the wound.

After twenty minutes of work, his eyelids fluttered open. I hadn't expected him to recover quite that soon, and I found myself staring into his eyes as the glaze cleared and he focused on my face.

"Wh-where..." he began.

I took his hand in mine as his father interrupted. "They're in the brig now, August. You don't have to worry anymore."

August didn't take his eyes off mine, but his fingers squeezed softly.

I heard a noise from behind, and turned to see the Commander standing up and walking towards the cot. "I think this is the first time we've all been together. Alone."

I dropped my gaze and just looked at August's pale hand, resting, cold, in mine.

What he would have said next I don't know. His wristcom beeped before he could say anything.

"Commander Howitz, the *Alacrity I* is closing to a thousand AUs."

"Keep up elusive maneuvers!" he growled into the speaker.

"But sir, there's more—our scopes just detected a transport from the cruiser *Comet III* following the *Alacrity I*."

My heart leapt. Crash was on his way! And he was bringing reinforcements!

"I'll be right there." Switching off the com, the Commander turned to us, his heavy brows furrowed. "Stay here. I'll be back when I've dealt with those imbeciles."

"Dealt with them?" I cried after him.

He called over his shoulder, "If he takes a hint, I won't kill him."

I believed him, and half-hoped Crash would take a hint. At the same time, I knew he wouldn't.

The Commander spent a moment at the locking panel by the door, and then left, sealing the door behind him. I knew him too well to think he'd assume we'd stay there without being forced, but still, I checked the door.

Locked. And no DNA clearance on this one. My clearance code didn't let me through either. He'd overridden everything.

"We can still save his life."

I didn't need to ask who August meant, and the thought made my heart sink through the floor. "His life. What life? He'll never be able to work again. Nothing will ever be the same."

He had pushed himself up into a half-sitting position, his elbows resting on the soft cot. "No. It won't."

I sat down on the floor, feeling like I should cry. It was no use. My eyes were dry—drier than I could ever remember them being. I felt nothing. I'd lost everything.

"You're a Christian aren't you?" he half-stated, rather timidly.

"Yes." There was a moment's silence. "Are you?"

"I don't know. I suppose so. But after mom died and you disappeared, I just..." He didn't finish his sentence. Instead, he started another. "I saw the Bible in your room when I was there. It was the first conventional book I'd seen on board, and when I walked over there I read the title."

"There's at least one more conventional book on board," I said, still feeling numb and heavy.

He looked at me quizzically.

"It's just like mine," I said. "It's the Doctor's."

"You're lucky you had him," he said. "I may not care much for what God did to us, but Dad outright hates Him."

"The same way he hates me," I whispered.

August said nothing. I dropped my gaze to the cold, white metal floor.

"Why are you asking me all this?" I asked.

"I just wondered if you were going to go on trusting God after all this. I mean, you liked your life before. But now that it's all gone..." He let his voice trail off.

My lips formed a yes, but the sound refused to follow. Of course I still trusted God. Didn't all things work together for good to those who loved Him? Couldn't I do all things through Him who strengthened me? Didn't those who waited on him mount up on wings as eagles? Wouldn't we have saved the Doctor by now if I hadn't been too stubborn to trust him before?

My gaze fell on the CMR scanner, laying uselessly by the cot where I'd scanned the Doctor a couple of nights before. I remembered him tossing it in the air just a few days ago, complaining about the dryers, bantering about the new uniforms.

In a few hours, I would be gone, the Doctor would be dead, and there would be someone else handling the scanner. Probably a nurse.

I couldn't say yes.

But I couldn't say no. That would deny everything I believed in.

So I said neither. Instead, I channeled all the energy I had left and stood slowly to my feet. "We have to get out of here. We have to save the Doctor."

"How?" August asked.

"I just know I'm not giving up on him now," I said. I looked at the CMR scanner again, and pictured it laying in a puddle of water in the sanitation room—

The sanitation room! *Andi, you're such a fool!*

"Come on!" I called, and began running towards the sanitation room.

"Where are you going?" he cried, standing up and starting my way, trying to keep up with me in his weakened state.

"To save the Doctor."

"How?" he panted.

I didn't know how. I just knew I had to.

Commander Howitz wasn't familiar with sickbay, he was too new to have used the sanitation room. Surely he hadn't thought of it. I raced down the curved row of sinks and dryers and, sure enough, found the door on the other end open.

August caught up with me as I paused at the opening and peered into the hall to make sure that no one was there.

"But what are you going to do?" he asked again.

"We can at least get the Doctor out," I said.

"Where is he?"

"He's on D-Deck, in Ensign Shelhammer's quarters."

"Guarded?"

"By two men."

He thought, still breathing heavily, for a moment. Then he looked at me.

"Didn't you say you got a galley assistant to help you with the generator?"

"Edwardo Sanchez," I nodded.

"And is he working there now?"

"I think so."

He thought for another moment, then spoke rapidly. "Most people don't know that I'm not in on this with my dad. Most people probably don't know the galley workers either. If we pretend to be a relief guard and send them to rest..."

"Yes!" I cried. "I'll find some way to get the machine, if you'll tell me what it looks like."

"It's the black, rectangular one, with a big gauge on the right and a silver switch and lots of dials."

"I remember it," I nodded. "I'll bring it to you..."

"In the hold. We'll be able to hide there."

"Hide in the provision section," I suggested. "Someone might see you if you hide in recycling."

"I'll be there." He laid a hand on my shoulder. "Are

you—sure you can do this?"

I pushed his hand away. I could feel his arm shaking, and it made me nervous. "I have to."

"Be careful."

"You, too. Now go, hurry!"

He took a deep breath and darted down the hall.

I started to step out, hesitated and closed my eyes. *I... trust you, God. I do. I do. Just please, please let this work. Let us save him. Even if... even if...* I choked. I couldn't go on. Opening my eyes, I started towards the elevator. "C-Deck," I said, not liking the way my voice shook. I had no plan. None at all. I just had to get inside that room again somehow.

I thought, harder and more desperately than I'd ever thought before, as I rode the elevator down and trotted down the hall. If I was lucky, I'd have the machine and be down in the hold before Commander Howitz even found that I'd left sickbay.

Of course, so far I hadn't been lucky at all. And there was one thing standing in the way—I had absolutely no way of getting into his quarters.

The walk to his door seemed both eternally long and impossibly short at the same time. When I finally reached it, I stood trembling at the door, thinking. If I could just figure out the code to his lock.

What could it be? It could be anything. I didn't know him well enough to know what he would use for a code.

"Genevieve Lavinia Sandison. You were named after her. Her!"

Her. The thing more important to him than any other in the world.

Her name must be Lavinia.

My fingers shaking so that they were almost uncontrollable, I turned on the keypad screen and typed in L-A-V-I-N-I-A.

An ugly beep sounded, and red letters flashed "Incorrect."

I stepped back. It had been a good try, but not good enough.

Lavinia. Lavinia. Sara.

Sara and Lavinia.

"Lavinia? What are you doing here? Where's Sara?"

Was that who the Doctor had mistaken me for when I visited him last night?

"Sara... Sara was my sister. You were her best friend. She had blonde hair and blue eyes."

The final piece of the puzzle fell in place. My mother and Crash's mother had been best friends.

It suddenly made perfect sense. She would have grown up in the same town with the Doctor's family. She would have watched him postpone college and career to take care of his little sister after his parents died. She would have known all about his devotion, his dedication, and his faith.

Who better to trust her daughter with?

"There you are."

The gravelly voice paralyzed me.

"Your precious Mr. Crash will reach us in a few minutes. We have to leave now." Gripping my arm, he started pulling me down the hall towards the airlock again.

"But..." I gasped, too shocked to do anything but run with him, "...you don't have access..."

"I finally managed to override it."

"August!" I cried.

"He'll have to come later."

I planted myself on the floor as best I could. "Please! Let me save the Doctor! I'll go with you... I'll do anything you want. Just..."

"We don't have time!" he growled, and with a wrench, he pulled me along again.

I wasn't going. Not when the Doctor was still in danger. August would be waiting for me in the hold, he wouldn't know that I wasn't coming with the machine.

I pulled away recklessly, knowing it would do no good. He kept pulling me along.

Just what was I going to do if I got free? He'd only catch me and get me, and take me with him again. I couldn't win. I wasn't strong enough.

No, I wasn't. But...

Taking only a second to plan, I stumbled forward and cried out, jerking him off balance for a moment. He let go of my arm for an instant, trying to right himself, and I ducked down, spun around, and started running.

"Stop!" he yelled.

I kept running, for all I was worth. I hadn't known my legs could move so fast, but I ran, ran, ran, hearing the pounding of his boots behind me. I had only a couple of yards on him, not enough to make it into the elevator before he could stop me.

I ran past the elevator and into the lounge, vaulting over the back of a couch and nearly collapsing when I dropped behind it, but I managed to keep going. In the back corner was the emergency pole, and I grabbed onto it, positioning my feet at the brim of the hole that led down to other levels.

I'd never tried this before. For half a second I hesitated, then I heard him bump into a small table and grunt.

I jumped into the hole, grabbing the pole with both hands.

Down I slid, trying to wrap my legs around the pole as well, but not managing it. A rough place caught my right hand, and I yelled at the pain as the skin was scraped off. Still I flew down, seeing levels pass in blurs of white. It was a good thing I wanted to go all the way to the bottom, because I had no idea how to stop at a level.

Before I'd even had time to take it in, I landed, my feet meeting the floor with an impact that shook my skeleton from tarsal bones to skull. Trying to think straight, I let go of the pole and threw myself backwards, so that I landed on my back on the floor.

A spasm of pain shot up my neck, but I stood up anyway, my knees feeling like jelly, and wobbled away from the pole.

I was in the brig, just where I'd wanted to be.

CHAPTER XXV

The long row of cells faced me, their purple-tinted energy shields sparkling and humming softly.

"What are you doing here?"

I snapped my head towards the noise, and saw Sigmet's face behind one of the shields.

Yes, he and Peat were both in the same cell. I rushed for it, hoping that Commander Howitz hadn't overridden the brig systems.

Reaching for the lock to their cell, I tried to speak calmly, but found my voice shaking. "You're right, he only wants me dead. He's chasing me now." Even as I entered the Doctor's emergency code into the lock, I heard the sound of someone sliding down the pole.

The lock flashed green, and the shield disappeared, leaving Peat and Sigmet free just as the Commander dropped skillfully to the ground, knees bent perfectly. He started forward, but Peat jumped to meet him, and the two huge men faced each other intently for half a second.

Then Peat reached for the Commander, who sidestepped and shot his fist towards Peat's chin.

I drew back. My idea was working! While they fought, I could slip away and hide, and maybe Crash would catch up with us. We still had time to save the Doctor's life.

I backed into something and grunted. Fingers gripped my arm, and I was yanked back. Before I could protest, a hand was clapped over my mouth.

Sigmet. But what—?

He pulled me backwards, and for an instant, I was too startled to struggle. By the time I began trying to pull away, he'd brought me out of the brig and into the hold. I reached up to pry his hand from my mouth, but he took it down himself, sealing the adjoining door with one hand, while still holding on to my arm.

The hold. We were in the hold.

"August!" I screamed, yanking away. "August, help! Edwardo, August, help me!"

Sigmet kept his grip on my arm and pulled me towards the wall on the opposite side of the room. "August!" I screamed again. He had to be down here.

"Andi?" a well-known accent replied.

I looked towards the provision shelves far to my left. A pale face with a crop of dark brown hair peeked around one of them.

"Andi! Stop!" he yelled, starting towards us.

But Sigmet stopped at the wall, and I looked forward to see what he was doing. The engineer's lift—he was taking me back up. To the airlock.

And the speeder was ready for takeoff.

"What about your boss?" I gasped as he flung open the little square door.

"Boss?" he asked, his odd, high eyes showing confusion.

"Leeke... isn't he your boss? Aren't you his assistant?"

Understanding flashed through his expression, and he smiled as he pushed me in. "I see. You think he's Leeke and I'm Mars. Well you have it backwards. He's not in charge—I am."

I could only stare. I had assumed—Peat was so big—

He climbed in after me, and I caught a glimpse of August running in our direction as Sigmet slammed the door closed and calmly ordered, "C-Deck."

The tiny lift started upwards, and I forced myself to calm. I wasn't going to give up now. I had to think clearly, find out how to get away from him.

He was the leader of the twosome—he was the one in

charge. He wasn't going to wait for his partner. He would save him later—or maybe not. Either way, he was taking me away with him now.

The lift stopped, and he slammed the door open, and pushed me roughly out into the fuel cell chambers in the front of the ship. It was dark there, and I stumbled through with his hand still clamping my shoulder. If only he were holding me a little more loosely, it might be possible to slip away in the shadows—

A twinge of pain pinched my knee, and I reflexively gripped it, but it died away just as his hand reached out in front of me and opened a door.

He still held tightly to my shoulder, and pushed me out. I didn't recognize the place where we were, it was dim and brown and dirty. A long metal walkway extended out from where we stood through the huge, cylindrical room we were in. Metal steps led up to a sold metal platform that stretched out before us, fenced in by railings.

A thruster. We were inside one of the thruster chambers that housed the mechanism for the thrusters that gave the ship its propulsion when not on warp speeds. A giant pipe came down from the ceiling and stretched all the way to the back of the ship—the thruster itself must be on the other side of the pipe.

Sigmet wasn't interested in going to the thruster. He continued to push me along, towards the stairs that went up and out of the thruster chamber.

I tried desperately to think. He was trying to lose Commander Howitz by taking a route he wouldn't expect. And he wouldn't expect it—he'd assume that Sigmet would take me the shortest way.

His hand loosened slightly for a second as he prepared to ascend the stairs, and I took the opportunity to duck away from his grasp, desperately. I dropped, landing in a sitting position on the solid metal platform below me, but I didn't take time to worry about the pain that crackled over my legs. I just started half-crawling, half-running back towards the lift. It probably wasn't the smartest place to go—but I had to go somewhere. I didn't have time to think.

My jacket was grabbed and yanked upward, and I found myself again in a fully standing position. Fingers wrapped around my arm until I let out a yelp of pain.

"Don't try that again," he said coolly, and began pulling me towards the stairs once more.

"Let go of her!" cried a gravelly voice from behind us.

I wouldn't have thought I would have been so glad to hear his voice again.

Of course, Sigmet didn't obey. He began pulling me up the stairs, but I reached down and held onto the metal railing. He kept dragging me, and my hands scraped across the rusty pipe. Flakes of metal dug into my skin and reopened the cut from my slide earlier.

I looked back in the direction the voice had come from. The Commander was jumping the last few steps up to the platform we'd just left. How had he figured out where I was?

Of course. The same way he'd figured out that I was on the *Surveyor* in the first place. The radialloy tracking device.

He took masterful leaps towards us. Sigmet pulled on me with a ferocity I hadn't seen from him before, and I screamed as my hands slid off the rail.

Unhindered, my captor rushed up the stairs at his top pace—but his odd, limping gait was ineffectual against the Commander's powerful strides. As much as I didn't want to go with him, I instinctively reached a bloody hand out to my father as he bounded up the steps. He took it and yanked me, so hard that I thought he must have pulled my shoulder from its socket.

Instead of freeing me, the yank sent Sigmet tumbling down the stairs with a yell, still hanging onto my other arm. I screamed again as the weight of the smaller man's body dragged me down and pulled my feet out from under me, but before I could land, the Commander put an arm around my waist and pulled me to my feet.

Sigmet lost his grip on me altogether, and slid down the stairs, letting out grunts and groans with every bump. I had no love for him, but still I winced when he landed at the bottom.

Before I had time to take in the fact that he was gone, the Commander began running up the stairs, this time with me in tow.

This apparently had not been such a good idea. This was just a game, they would keep on trading me violently back and forth forever—unless one of them defeated the other, in which case I'd be stuck in the speeder with whoever won, on my way to certain death, knowing that I'd left the Doctor insane with no one to care for him.

I had to keep them fighting—if they kept at it long enough, it might be enough time for Crash to come aboard, and then someone might be able to find me and save me.

I braced my tired body to begin struggling again, when I heard a great thumping on the metal slats behind me. Before either I or the Commander could turn around, iron fingers gripped my shoulders and pulled me back. Peat.

Though appearing startled, the Commander retained his hold on me, and again my arm was pulled so hard that I thought it would be pulled off.

I screamed. "Stop! Stop!"

CHAPTER XXVI

"Two against one, Sandison!" puffed Sigmet's voice. I couldn't see past Peat's giant body, but I heard boots tapping on the steps and knew that the scientist must be running up the stairs. "Give her up!"

"Give up my daughter?" growled the Commander.

Peat scoffed. "You're not fooling anybody. You never wanted her."

"I have the legal right to her!"

Neither of the other men apparently thought this worthy of an answer. Peat and the Commander glared into each other's eyes for a moment, while Sigmet limped up and stood panting beside his assistant.

There was an awful silence. Peat's hands were still clamped on my shoulders, while the Commander held my arm in a vice-like grip. For the first time I noticed the clanking, methodical, echoey clanking, from far below us. The hold was a straight drop down, I realized—with the great metal crushing bins that consolidated our recycling directly below.

Commander Howitz let go of my arm, and at the same time drew his blaster from its holster and pointed it at Peat. "All right then."

Peat pulled me close to him and forced me between himself and the blaster.

The Commander shook his head. "I'll shoot, Mars, you know I will. She's as good to me dead as alive."

The words, together with the cold, gravelly tone in which

they were spoken, forced a hard, short shiver through my body, prickling my skin with goosebumps.

"I forgot that you only play the loving father card when it suits you," scoffed Peat, pushing me away from him. I grunted as I landed on my hands and knees, hair falling into my face. As my torn hands hit the ground, I bit my lip to keep from screaming.

"Impasse," Peat's strong voice said, and I looked back at him. His own blaster pointed now at Commander Howitz. He must have drawn it as he pushed me away.

I was free. But if I tried to move, they'd both shoot me. I had no doubt of it. My own father had said it, they didn't need me alive.

Crash, Crash, come on, please find me!

"We're wasting our time!" Peat shouted.

"Listen, Sandison," Sigmet said evenly. "We're not going to get anywhere this way. We pretended to agree to a settlement before— to split the profits—why not agree to it for real? We can all get away in the speeder."

"I don't trust him," Peat protested before the Commander could answer.

"A truce then," Sigmet suggested. "We can at least get away from here and fight about this later. If we don't get off soon, none of us will get the alloy."

I watched the Commander's face, my heart thumping loud and fast. He considered—

A huge red light on a control panel near us blinked on and off, and at the same time an ear-splitting beep echoed through the thruster chamber.

"Thrusters engaging," came a computerized voice, as the blinking and beeping continued, "in five, four, three..."

Commander Howitz dropped to the floor. A blaster fired, and I saw a small burst of energy shoot over my head.

"...two, one."

A roaring thundered above us, and the air immediately began getting hot. The floor rumbled, vibrated, and then heaved, sending Peat and Sigmet stumbling towards the panel.

Now was my chance.

I tried to get to my feet, but the metal walkway heaved again, throwing me chest first to the ground. I gasped as all the air shot from my lungs, but I didn't dare wait to get my breath. Panting for air, I got to my knees and began crawling back towards the lift. If I could just get there—

The floor lurched again, as the roaring continued, and my injured hands skidded across the floor. I kept going, gasping for breath and in pain as each hand touched the hard metal. I heard yells from behind me, but didn't dare look back.

The air was getting hotter. Already sweat was dripping down my face and back, but I kept going.

Another lurch hurled me against the railing, driving the vertical pole between my ribs. I cried out and tightened my muscles, gripping wildly for the railing above me.

"Get down, you fools!" I heard someone yell.

Another violent lurch threw my legs over the edge of the platform, and I screamed as I felt my body slide to follow it. I clawed uselessly at the floor, then grabbed for the railing.

I found it just as my cheek slammed against the edge of the platform, and I gripped it with both bleeding hands. Gravity jerked at me, straining my already-tired shoulder joints.

And I hung, panting.

Everything kept on shaking. My eyes were almost on a level with the platform, but I could see Peat and Sigmet holding onto the blinking thruster panel, and the Commander crawling, stumbling towards them.

What was he doing? Did they even notice I was gone?

It was then that I looked up and saw an opening in the pipe. A section of it near the wall was removed, leaving a yawning gap. The malfunctioning thruster—it was being repaired.

I felt blood ooze from my hands onto the pole, making it harder to keep my grip. I screamed as I felt one hand slip, and slid it over the rusty metal to a dryer spot.

"Andi!"

Where had that voice come from? And was it...

It was Crash! From my wristcom!

I couldn't answer—even if my hands had been free, my com still wasn't transmitting.

"Andi, I tracked you on the screen. I'm coming right now to get you."

A computerized voice made another announcement that I could only make out part of. "Warning...online...vacate..."

I heard the Commander scream, "You fools!"

My hands slipped again.

I felt almost insane with fear. The clanking blackness yawned below me like a maw, threatening to swallow me the moment I lost my grip.

"Father!" I screamed, but he didn't even hear me. He was still trying to make his way to the panel.

I struggled to pull myself up, straining every muscle in my body, pulling, pulling on the bar, but I couldn't do it.

My wristcom beeped again. "Andi, I'm almost there!" Crash again. He was coming. He would save me, and everything would be all right. Everything would be fine.

"Andi," came a deeper voice. One I recognized. Guilders. "*Let go.* Let go, now."

I froze, and time froze with me, as my mind screamed in terror. Let go? What was he saying? Was he *insane*? I'd be crushed—killed! Crash would be here soon—

Let go.

If I'd let go of my doubt and trusted the Doctor days ago, none of this would have happened.

If I'd trusted God with my life, if I'd *let it go*, the Doctor would still be sane.

The Doctor had never failed me. Neither had God.

Neither had Guilders.

A louder rumbling opened up above my head, and I heard a clanking, drowning out that from below. The three men struggled over the platform, screaming things I couldn't hear.

Closing my eyes tight, I let go.

I plummeted, and a single second after the metal had slipped from my fingers, a fountain of flames shot over the platform out of the opening of the pipe. Simultaneously, a metal casing clanked down and fitted over the platform where I had hung just a moment before, shutting off the flames, and three distinct screams of agony followed me as I tumbled down into the blackness.

I didn't have time to scream or cry, or even think. I was falling—soon I'd be crushed in the giant recycling bins.

But for now—for this second—I was free. I was flying.

My heart cried, tears I couldn't associate with either joy or sorrow. It just cried.

And then for an instant I saw the provision shelves ahead of me, far away, and before I could think, I landed, landed in something soft and downy, something that cradled me as I sank into it, gently supporting me and cushioning my slow descent.

Then I stopped.

For an instant, I wondered if I'd died, and I was laying on the floor of Heaven. Blackness loomed above me. I was shaken, and my neck hurt a little, but that was all, and I could see whiteness in my peripheral vision.

My father was dead.

The Doctor was insane.

My heart ached at both thoughts and yet—I rested. I could rest now.

Peace flooded me.

"Andi!"

Before I could react, a pair of arms had scooped me up, and I was pressed to a rough jacket. I could hear a warm heart beating beneath my ear, and the arms held me as if they'd never let me go.

"Dad?" I gasped. "Doctor?"

It couldn't be his voice. He was dead—he had to be.

"You're safe," he whispered, and his hands stroked my hair.

"Is she all right, Gerry?"

My heart still wasn't allowing me to believe that it was him. I pulled away from the arms, and looked up into the face that belonged to the heart.

It was his face. Tired, but intelligent, sane. Smiling. Love shining from the gray eyes, face and hands dry once again. "Are you all right?"

I touched his cheek with my forefinger. "You—you were insane. It was too late."

"No," he said softly, taking my hand. "He lied, to speed things up."

Then, I understood. We'd had more than twenty hours all along.

"Did it work, Doctor Lloyd?" I heard an Austrian accent ask pantingly. "Is she all right?"

The softness. They'd put something in the bin to break my fall, and left Guilders, the only one with a working wristcom, to tell me what to do.

If I hadn't let go, I'd be dead.

A sob escaped me, and I buried my face in his jacket.

He kept on stroking my hair, letting me weep against the rough, comfortable fabric of his uniform.

CHAPTER XXVII

My memories of what happened after that are fuzzy. I remember waking up on a cot in sickbay, with the nice, familiar, humming of a monitor beside me.

At first I didn't move, then I heard a voice speaking nearby. My ears were still having trouble functioning, but I strained them to hear.

"...a couple ccs should do it. You'll need some rest, my boy." The most beloved voice in my world.

"Doctor?" I called, starting to raise myself on one elbow.

"Give him the shots for me," I heard him say, then he hastened to my side. I let myself drop back onto the cot, and stared back at his face, still not taking in the fact that he was alive and well.

He smiled at me for a moment, his hands in the pockets of his white coat, then he leaned down and kissed me gently on the forehead. "How are you doing?"

I inhaled deeply. "I'm okay. I'm a little sore."

Pulling my hands up to look at them, I saw that they were nearly healed, with just some clear dressing wrapped around them to hold everything in place while the regeneration continued to take effect. "What happened? How did you..." I couldn't figure out how to ask it.

With a slight sigh, he sat on the edge of my cot. "I don't remember much of what happened in the past few days. Trent and Guilders filled me in some. Apparently while Guilders was trying to find you, Ralston and Lieutenant How... August managed to override the security in Howitz's door. He'd rigged it with an alarm, but he couldn't hear it in the thrusters."

So that was how he'd figured out where I was when I tried my mother's name in his cabin lock.

"And... you know who he was? You know about August and... the radialloy?"

"Trent told me." He laid his hand over mine. "I'm so sorry you had to go through all that without me." There was silence for a minute, then he said, more gruffly, "If I wasn't such a grumpy old man, I'd say I was proud of you."

I smiled. "You're not a grumpy old man, dad."

"Then I suppose I will say it."

I reached up and put my arms around his neck. He hugged me back, and we stayed like that for a long time.

Finally he laid me back down. "It's over now. They all died in the accident—one of them bumped the thruster controls and turned it back on while the something-or-other was open."

I sighed. I should have been glad he was gone, glad that I'd never hear that gravelly voice again, but I felt strangely heavy. "Dad... you know who my mother was?"

He was silent for a moment. Then he said, "I found the picture in your jacket pocket. Lavinia."

"She was your sister's best friend, wasn't she? Crash's mother and my mother. That's why Crash thought he recognized August. He'd known the family when he was little."

The Doctor nodded. "She was a beautiful woman. A brave woman. Like you, Andi."

I couldn't think of anything to say. I swallowed, and remembered something. "And... Doctor Holmes?"

"I have to assume that..." he stopped.

"My father killed him."

He nodded again. "He must have tracked you to Emmett somehow, and used that—that memory machine to get him to tell that we were in space."

And he'd left Doctor Holmes to die. I shuddered, and the

Doctor held my hand more tightly.

One thing still did not make sense to me. "Dad?"

He looked at me.

"That day—when Crash left. When it all started... you said that you needed to test me for something, but you never did it."

I let my question go unspoken.

He sighed, and winced as if it hurt to remember. "Your father had come into my room the night before, carrying a box with him. I know now that that must have been when he..."

I closed my eyes and nodded.

The Doctor cleared his throat and went on. "At the time though, he said that it was something he needed to implement into sickbay for engineering. He tried to act like it was only a business visit—but I sensed some kind of... resentment."

I knew what he meant, and wondered now if that hidden anger was what had always made me uncomfortable around him.

"Anyway, he made some remark about you not being able to go down into engineering. It was offhand, and I can't even remember exactly what he said, but his tone—his attitude—it was like he was probing. I didn't like it, especially with what had happened to your knee earlier, so—I decided I had to figure out once and for all what that metal was." He paused for awhile. "I guess we know now what it was."

Nodding, I could only say, "I guess we do."

In the silence that followed, I remembered my brother. "Where's August?" I asked. "Is he okay?"

"He'll be all right. Blood pressure has come back to a safe level, but we're going to have to do something to help him if he's going to be working here in this stress factory. Incorporate more sodium into his diet, lay off the carbohydrates, you know how it goes."

I understood all this about blood pressure and sodium, but that wasn't what I was asking. "I know, Dad, but—how *is* he?"

The Doctor turned to look over his shoulder at the cot where August lay, then turned back to me with a helpless expression. "If you're feeling all right, I think you should go talk to him."

I knew that expression. He might be able to diagnose heart disease, set broken arms and cure dyspepsia, but when it came to comforting people, he was lost. Somehow he never knew what to say. And while his gruff bedside manner could serve to inspire a mysterious confidence in the sick in body, it did nothing for the sick at heart. And that was what August must be now.

The Doctor rose, and I sat up slowly. Finding that I could move all right, I stood, and made my way to the cot where my brother lay.

He lay motionless, staring at the bleak, white ceiling without expression. His hands were folded over his chest, and the color hadn't come back into his face.

I knelt beside him. "Are you feeling better?"

He didn't answer, or even indicate that he'd heard me.

I lay my hand over his. "August, I'm sorry..."

He turned slowly to face me. "Your Book is right, Andi."

"What do you mean?"

"That conventional Book of yours."

"I thought you said you didn't really..."

"I know what I said. But since he died... things are different. To you, he was just a cruel, heartless man, and he was all that, but—he was still my dad. I remember him teaching me things, helping me, picking me up when I fell, as a little boy. Underneath it all—I don't know. He always was still that man to me."

"But... what does that have to do with my book?" A tear rolled down my face, and I squeezed his hand.

"Your Book says that 'the wages of sin is death, but the gift of God is eternal life.' Dad didn't have that gift. I know he didn't."

"And do you?"

"Maybe. But he's the one that's dead. He's the one that's gone, not me. Why would God take him before he was ready, Andi?" Moisture stood in his brown eyes as he looked into mine.

I knew I had no answer to that question. But now, I knew I didn't need one. Because it didn't matter anymore.

"August—I don't know. I know this won't sound helpful, but—you just have to trust. Because 'all things work together for good to them that love God.' He's never failed me, August. He won't fail you."

"But what if I don't love Him?"

"Then you'd better start," I said, laying my other hand over his. "You didn't die, August. You didn't lose your life. You have me, you have a new life ahead of you."

He was silent, and his face didn't change. I didn't know if he was taking my words to heart or not, but there was one more thing I had to say. "And... you want to know one good thing I see from this? Your change of heart. God is calling to you, August. Whether you like it or not, He's calling to you."

Brushing my hand over his, I stood up and turned away from him. Maybe my words had helped him, maybe not. I longed for him to have the peace I felt, but I was sure that my words were true, and I trusted God to do the rest.

As I started towards the hall, to get some rest in my cabin, I saw someone coming out of the sanitation room.

It was a young woman, slender, probably six or seven years older than myself, rubbing some sanitizer between her hands. A white medical tunic covered her *Surveyor* uniform, and her armband bore the red cross insignia that I knew signified nurses.

Her skin was a rich olive, and her hair, which fell in waves to her shoulders, was dark, like her large eyes.

She smiled at me, and the Doctor stepped to my side.

"Andi," he explained. "This is Olive McMillan. Engineer McMillan got back from his honeymoon leave—just in time, too. His wife signed on to help, and since she's an R.N., Trent thought she could be useful to me."

The beautiful girl smiled again, and held out her slender hand. "It's lovely to meet you, Andi."

For an instant, I hesitated. Then I gave a return smile, and put my own hand out. "I'm glad to meet you. It will be good to have some more help around here."

It was hard for me to say it, and to sound genuine. I still didn't want a stranger in sickbay. But somehow, even though I still didn't like the idea, I felt resigned. It was for the best.

The only indication of understanding that the Doctor gave was to put his arm around my shoulders for a moment, but it was enough for me.

It was time to let go.

A beep came from my wristcom, followed by the Captain's voice. "Andi, are you there?"

"Yes, Captain."

"Come on up to the bridge, I want to show you something."

I smiled up at the Doctor. "Care to come along?" I asked.

For answer, he held out his arm. As I took it, he said to the nurse, "You can let the boy go. But he's off duty for forty-eight hours."

"Yes, Doctor," the girl nodded. Then she smiled a full, genuine smile at me. "I hope we'll be friends."

I smiled back. "I hope so, too."

Then she scurried off, and the Doctor and I left sickbay together.

When we walked through the sliding doors that led to that always exciting room, I looked around contentedly. There sat the Captain, giving orders commandingly, there was Guilders, obeying staunchly. And Crash sat in the visitor's seat, his boots propped up on the comm marshal's console. As we entered, he turned, grinned, and saluted, and I smiled. It was good to have him back.

The Captain turned and saw us before we could announce our presence, and he smiled. "Ah Andi, Gerry." He stood up and walked over to me, taking my free hand kindly in both of his. "How are you feeling?"

"Just fine, Captain. What was it you wanted to show me?"

"We're approaching the Artemis Nebula, and I thought you'd like to see. I know you always like looking at the nebulas."

"Yes I do! Thank you for thinking of me."

With a charismatic smile, he tipped his cap to me, shook the Doctor's hand warmly, and returned to his chair. Guilders turned and winked—actually winked—at me, filling me with a glad warmth. I owed him a lot of gratitude.

As we came in sight of the enormous nebula, I drew closer to the Doctor gladly. It was beautiful, with its misty, shifting clouds of purple and pink, ever moving gently like the northern lights of Earth. I smiled.

I heard the bridge doors slide open, but didn't turn to see who entered. And yet somehow, I was not surprised when August quietly approached and stood beside me. Together, the three of us—myself, my brother, and the Doctor—gazed at the beauty spread out before us in the star-studded blackness.

Then August spoke softly, so softly that no one but myself could have heard him. "The heavens declare the glory of God, and the firmament shows his handiwork."

I linked my arm through his, wordlessly, as the *Surveyor* made her way into the outer reaches of God's creation.

Did you read the bonus prologue online before reading this book?

Now it's time to continue Harry's story.

To read the epilogue, go to:
http://jgracepennington.com/radialloy-epilogue/
and type in this code:

KAINUSGE

About the Author

J. Grace Pennington has been telling stories since she could talk, and writing them down since age five. Now she lives in the Texas Hill Country with her parents, her eight younger siblings, and her horse, Pioneer. When she's not writing, she enjoys reading good books, playing movie soundtracks on the piano, and looking up at the stars.

You can find out more about her writing, including the Firmament series, at www.jgracepennington.com.

Made in the USA
Lexington, KY
18 July 2012